TONY SAVALA

by
Dorothy Hamilton
Illustrated by James Ponter

HERALD PRESS, SCOTTDALE, PENNSYLVANIA

White dove, white dove,
Tell me if you please,
Where were you traveling,
Your route so straight, your heart at ease.

From my country
I departed with the thought of
seeing Spain.
I flew as far as the Pyrenees,
There lost my pleasure
And found pain. *

Robert Laxalt

*Dove Song from "The Land of Ancient Basques," Robert Laxalt
National Geographic, Vol. 134: no. 2: Aug.: p. 243.

1

Tony Savala couldn't get to sleep. He'd doubled his pillow and thumped it to make the feathers fluffy. This didn't help. Then he threw it to the foot of the bed, but he was still awake.

Now Tony lay facing the wide window, his head on the crook of his elbow. The streetlights made the night almost as light as day. But the world and life seemed dark and gloomy to Tony.

He could hear the familiar sounds of home. Cars hummed along the highway four blocks away. Music from someone's radio drifted in the open window. His dog Lucky was barking at something from the backyard.

"What'll I be hearing this time tomorrow night? Dumb old sheep, probably. Maybe coyotes or wolves or whatever animals live in the Sierra Nevada Mountains."

Tony had heard stories of the Basque sheepherders for as many of his thirteen years as he could remember. His father had grown up in the foothills of the East Humboldt range of the mountains. And Tony's grandfather, Ascona Savala, still tended a flock of sheep and lived alone in a small camp wagon. Tony was going to spend a whole month there.

Tony didn't like the idea of wasting four whole weeks in a sheep camp. For one reason he didn't know his grandfather. It would be like living with a stranger.

5

Tony had kept trying to get out of going. He'd said over and over that this might be the year he'd get to represent Meadow Lark Pool in the all-city swim meet. Besides that, the coach of the Little League team was counting on him to play second base.

No one had paid much attention to Tony's reasons. His parents sort of flicked them off as they would a June bug that landed on their wrists.

Tony had made his next to last try a week before. He and his dad were dividing the clumps of iris roots. They put some in a new bed along the garage. They carried others over to the new church on the edge of the housing addition.

The sun was like gold behind the gray stone church. The gleaming spire seemed to be reaching toward heaven.

The pastor helped them set out the knobby roots. "Won't they need water or peat moss or plant food?" Pastor Miller asked.

"Not iris," Joe Savala said. "They're a hardy flower. They remind me of us Basque. You can move us, transplant us, and even freeze us but we survive."

Pastor Miller smiled. "The spirit is strong but some of us are better instruments than others." Then he put his hand on Tony's shoulder. "I hear you will soon know more of your ancestry, Anthony. Right?"

"Yes, sir," Tony said. But there was no enthusiasm in his voice.

Evening shadows were creeping across the green lawns and wide sidewalks as Tony and his father walked home.

Big Joe cleared his throat and said, "I hoped I wouldn't have to say what you're about to hear. But I'll speak only once on this subject. You're dragging your feet about this trip, making your mother sad and me — well, I'm disappointed."

"Disappointed? Why?"

"Well, this trip is really a gift, a rather expensive package."

"But I didn't ask for — "

"I know! I know! But this is the point. I'm a Basque at heart, and your granddad is a sheepherder. He came from the Pyrenees Mountains more than fifty years ago. He's a strong and brave man. I want you to know him. It's that simple."

Tony knew better than to say what he was thinking. What was so great about being a sheepherder? Would a really strong man live in a small camp wagon all alone except for a bunch of clunky sheep?

Tony had seen his grandfather once. Ascona Savala had visited his son in Indianapolis when Tony was six. In the boy's memory the sturdy Basque had wide shoulders, a deep suntan, and spoke very few words. His hair was the color of pepper and salt mixed together.

Tony's mother had told her son about the Basque sheepherders before her husband's father arrived. "When you're older you'll want to read about them for yourself."

"What's a Basque?" Tony asked.

"They're people who live in or come to this country from a mountain land shared by France and Spain."

"Why?" Tony asked.

"Why?" Jane Savala said. "To tend sheep. That's what they seem to know best; better than any other people in the world."

"Is my daddy a Basque?"

"Well, he's always lived in this country. But he's been a sheepherder — when he wasn't in school in Winnemucca and in college."

"Then how come he's here?" Tony asked.

"Because your grandfather saved his money — enough to send your father to college in Denver. Then he met me, was offered a job at the transformer plant and here we are."

"Did Granddad want Daddy to come so far away?" Tony had asked.

"Probably not," Jane Savala said. "I often feel guilty because we don't see him often. But he never complained or made us feel that we should settle down near him."

Tony remembered that they sent big boxes to Nevada at Christmas and sometimes during the year. And every time pictures were taken at school Jane had one enlarged to send to the sheep camp. Big Joe teased her, saying, "Father's probably papered the walls of the camp wagon with our Tony's face."

Tony did all this remembering before he and his father reached the backyard of their home. He knew what his dad meant. But he still didn't want to go. Summer was so great in Candlewood Hills he didn't want to leave.

Tony started up the flagstone walk. His shoulders slumped. He'd about given up hope of getting out of going.

"One more thing, Anthony."

Oh boy! When he calls me Anthony the law is being laid down.

Tony stopped but didn't turn to face his father. Joe Savala walked around to a spot in front of the dejected, moody boy.

"I've felt you look down on your grandfather because of his occupation."

Tony didn't know what to say. He dug the toe of his left sneaker into the clipped grass along the walk.

"Let me tell you, Son. Any work which is honorable is to be respected."

"But, Dad, how much money does a shepherd earn?"

Joe Savala's face got red all the way up to his black hair. "That's another reason I want you to go. Money's not a fair yardstick. I know it seems like everyone measures men and life by how much money is earned or spent. But there's more to living than a race to grab. I hope you see what I mean before you board the plane to come home."

"Oh boy," Tony thought. "This is one of those things that's supposed to be good for me. They usually are a dull drag."

Jane Savala came to the screen door. "Come on in, you two. I have tall ice cream floats ready for you."

"What're you trying to do? Fill Tony up with ice cream. Give him a month's supply?"

Jane smiled. "Maybe. He probably won't have a chance to buy any."

"He might. Dad goes into Winnemucca for supplies now and then. And other herders from various camps stop by. Tony might want to ride with them."

From that evening up until the morning of the day he was to leave Tony hadn't openly objected to going to Nevada. The plane ticket was in his dad's wallet. Arrangements had been made for his grand-dad to meet the bus at Winnemucca.

Sometimes Tony had heard his father and mother make plans for his summer as if he weren't there. But he was honest enough to admit that they'd tried to get him interested. They probably think I'm pouting, he often thought. I guess I am, a little. But they go on getting all excited about it — like they're glad to get rid of me. When this thought came to Tony's mind he had another reason for not talking. There was a big lump in his throat. Words couldn't get around it.

2

Tony turned over and lay on his back but he didn't feel comfortable in that position either. "Maybe if I shut the blinds and make the room dark I won't keep seeing pictures in my mind."

As he walked to the window he saw his open suitcase on the big red hassock. His mother had said that morning, "I'll leave it open until the last minute. You may want to put something in yourself."

She had brought a stack of clean T-shirts to Tony's room that morning just as he was ready to go down to breakfast.

He stood at the door and watched as his mother arranged things. She tucked socks and small articles of clothing in the ends, filling in the space beyond the new riveted blue jeans and sweatshirts.

She seems real cheerful about all this, Tony thought as he watched.

"I have another last-minute packing job to do," Jane Savala said. "I bought a new gym bag yesterday. You'll need it for school anyway. I'm putting in some surprises for you and Father Savala."

The only surprise I want is to be told I can stay at home.

His mother went on talking, saying things Tony'd already heard four or five times and hadn't wanted to hear in the first place.

"It's like your father said. It's cold out there at night even if it is June. That's why we bought the

11

quilted jacket. And you remember of course, that your sleeping bag should be waiting at Winnemucca for grandfather to pick up. We ordered it in plenty of time. It'd be too bulky for you to take on the plane."

"I remember," Tony said.

Tony started down the curving stairs. He'd thought a little about going over to Rod's or Allen's. But they'd been a little nasty the night before, teasing him about being a nursemaid to a lamb and stuff like that. At least Tony hoped they were just kidding around. *Anyway, they've probably made other plans — like I'm already gone.*

"I'm going out in the backyard and transplant some snapdragons. Would you hook up the hose, please, and drag it over to me?" Mrs. Savala said. "After I fix your breakfast."

"Sure, Mom," Tony answered. "But I don't want much to eat. Just juice and maybe some cookies. I don't feel very hungry."

Jane Savala looked at her son and started to speak. Then she quickly turned away.

It turned out that Tony was a lot hungrier than he'd thought. His appetite wouldn't let him stage a hunger strike. He ate three pieces of toast spread with strawberry-pineapple jam.

The sun was silvery bright that morning. Tony blinked as he walked out the door. The sky was a sea of blue except for a few woolly white clouds. They looked a little like clustered sheep. Didn't everything these days?

Tony pulled the reel of plastic hose over to where his mother knelt. He watched her hollow out a place for the tender plants and then cover them gently around the hair-like roots. She didn't wear gloves like Rod's mother. Jane Savala liked the feel of the earth.

Tony looked all around. "Maybe I'm trying to take pictures with my mind. So I can see home while I'm out in the rocky land. So I can see this place while I'm not here."

All at once Tony felt like crying even if he was too old. *Maybe that makes me a baby — a thirteen-year-old infant.*

Instead he blurted out the words, "Why do I have to go on this clunky old trip?"

Jane sat back on her heels and looked up at her son. Then she patted the ground and said, "Sit down, please. I'll try to make you understand."

Tony pulled a blade of grass and wound it around his thumb as his mother spoke, gently, softly.

"I've tried to stay out of this, let this be between you and your father. But evidently you haven't understood."

"Yes, I have," Tony answered. "Dad wants me to know Granddad, and learn to appreciate my origins. But I still don't want to go. Maybe this origin bit doesn't mean much to me. Does it to you, Mom? Really?"

Tears filled Jane Savala's eyes as she reached over and rubbed Tony's wrist with one finger. "It might not if I didn't know your father and didn't realize how much he loves his dad. You see, there was too little caring in my family. My parents were divorced. I never felt much security until I met Joseph Savala. I never went to church until then."

13

"Why do I have to go on this clunky trip?"

"You didn't?"

"No. No one took me or even cared enough to send me."

"I didn't know that," Tony said.

"Well, it's true. And this is what I mean or what your father means. His strength and qualities of character are the result of his upbringing. He wants you to have a taste of that kind of experience. Won't you try to understand, Tony? We don't want you to be gone from us. It'll be so lonely here — " Her voice faltered.

Tony felt a little better. He saw a little more sense in his father's reason for sending him to Nevada. He began to realize his parents weren't trying to get rid of him. He'd be missed.

The rest of the day went surprisingly fast. Tony fixed the loose boards on Lucky's doghouse and greased his Sting Ray bike. Later he and his mother went to the supermarket and to a drive-in for lunch.

Jane showed Tony the things she was putting in the new gym bag. There were packages of cheese crackers, candy bars, paperback books, and a small transistor radio. "I've also filled a plastic box with butterscotch brownies. I remember how well Father Savala liked them when he was here."

Jane went on to say that her husband had teased her about putting in books. "He said you wouldn't have much time for reading. None by day. And that you'd be too tired to read much at night."

Tony had wondered then as he did now in bed. "What'll I be doing to make me *that* tired?"

Suddenly he began to yawn and within a few

minutes he was in a deep sleep. He dreamed that he was lost in the mountains. The wind howled and snow swirled all around him. He was shaking with cold. Then he opened his eyes to see his father's face. "Get up, Son," Joe Savala said as he shook Tony's arm. "We have only an hour and ten minutes to get to the airport."

Tony was glad that he didn't really get wide awake until he'd been up about an hour. This way he felt a little numb. He dressed, ate, and left the house in a kind of haze. It was easier that way.

He'd zipped the gym bag shut the last thing before he left the room. His father had taken the heavy suitcase downstairs. As Tony pushed down on the bag of brownies he saw his red leather Bible at the side of the bag. Under it was a booklet of daily devotions, the kind the Savalas read the mornings they ate breakfast together. *Mom's like that. She wouldn't preach at me about keeping on with the daily reading. But she'd see that I have what I need.*

No one said much on the way to the airport. Everything had already been discussed. Tony looked for friends as they drove down Kimberly Lane and on out of Candlewood Hills. But it was too early for any of them to be out.

The plane left Indianapolis on schedule. Tony was glad. Standing around would have made the good-byes harder. As it was no one cried except Jane Savala. "But that's OK," Tony thought. "I'd feel funny if Mother didn't cry."

Joe Savala put his arm around Tony's shoulders as they walked to the big gate. "Now remember,

Son. Go to the information desk in Elko. They'll tell you how to get to the bus station."

Suddenly Tony felt a little panicky. "But if I don't know when the bus leaves Elko for Winnemucca how will Grandfather know when to meet me?"

"Don't worry. He'll be there. He knows when the jet gets to Elko. The ticket agent will tell him when the next bus leaves there. See?"

"Yes, I see," Tony said. He gave his mother a last quick hug and said good-bye again to his dad.

He didn't look back again until he was seated on the plane. He picked out his parents by looking for his mother's pink dress. That was the last thing he saw before the jet roared down the runway.

3

Tony had never ridden on a jet. He'd been out to Weir Cook Airport several times, and taken two rides in a smaller plane with some of the boys of Boy Scout Troop No. 12. So he wasn't scared during takeoff, at least not much.

As the big silver plane soared into the blue sky Tony looked at the other passengers. Everyone acted as if they rode on a jet every day. *It's probably just like a bus ride to them.*

The lady who sat next to Tony smiled and offered him a pink peppermint. She told him she was a schoolteacher in a little town called Farmland.

"I thought that was just the name for fields," Tony said. "Where corn and tomatoes grow."

"It is," the lady said. "But with a capital letter it's the name of the town where I live. That way it spells home to me. I guess I'm a little homesick already. I don't go away very often."

Tony was wondering why she was making the trip. Who would tell a grown-up schoolteacher to go anyplace. *I guess she's not supposed to learn about her origins. They're back where she came from.*

The blue-eyed lady must have read Tony's mind. "My oldest daughter lives in California. She has a new baby. That's why I'm making this trip."

Tony told his seatmate a little about why he was going to Nevada. But he didn't say that his grandfather was a sheepherder.

18

The stewardess served a light lunch at eleven. "We'll be landing at Elko in forty-five minutes," she told Tony. "You have plenty of time before the bus leaves for Winnemucca."

Tony began to feel scared. He had a little trouble swallowing his lettuce and ham sandwich. The lemonade and chocolate sundae went down easier.

The lady from Farmland said, "Why don't you take your sandwich with you. You might get hungry on the bus."

"That's a good idea," Tony said. "Thanks."

"And why don't you take my pear?" the lady said. "I never eat this much food at one time."

Tony felt a little sad when the stewardess told the passengers to fasten their seat belts for landing. She and the lady from Farmland had made him feel comfortable. *Now I'll be all alone again.*

Tony began to wonder where the bus station was and if he'd have to walk — or run — to get there.

Just then the pretty black-haired stewardess tapped his shoulder. "Is someone meeting you here?"

"No, ma'am," Tony said. "I'm going on to a place called Winnemucca, by bus. If I find it!"

"I see. Well, I tell you what! If you'll wait until the passengers have left the plane I'll go to the ticket office with you and we'll find out where the bus station is."

"Will that take long?" Tony asked.

"Not too long," she said.

Within a few minutes they'd found the small square bus depot and Tony bought his ticket. The agent told Tony he'd be leaving for Winnemucca in thirty minutes.

"How about going across the street to the drugstore with me?" she said. "We both have a half hour to wait."

They looked at postcards and Tony bought five. Then he saw a rack which held small bottles of hand lotion. He bought one and gave it to the stewardess. "That's for helping me," he said.

"Well, thank you," the stewardess said. "Now you have a good summer." Then she headed back up the street.

Tony bought three candy bars before he boarded the bus. He also had time to write a message to his parents on one of the cards.

There were only four other people on the rumbling brown bus. Two looked as if they could be cowboys except that they didn't wear holsters and guns as one sees in the movies.

Both young men wore high nail-studded boots. They pulled wide-rimmed hats down over their eyes and slept most of the way.

The man across the aisle had very black hair and skin the color of malted milk. *I wonder if he's an Indian?*

Tony turned sidewise and looked out the window. He saw uneven mountains all along the skyline. Their slopes were dusted with snow. Pine trees which looked like tall and ragged feathers dotted the foothills.

"It's a lot different from Indiana. Like another world," Tony thought. He leaned his head back on the bumping seat and began to feel a little sleepy. "But if I doze off I may not know when we get to Winnemucca."

Long purple shadows were creeping across the snowy mountain slopes when the bus pulled up to the long low station. Tony looked out the window. "Will Grandfather know me? I'm not sure I'll know him."

Then he saw a man standing in the center of the narrow sidewalk. *It's Granddad! Just as I remember him.*

Ascona Savala wore a gray cotton shirt, open at the neck. The wide rim of his black felt hat rolled up at the sides. A band of silver and blue ran around the dented crown.

Tony drew a long breath, stood up and reached for his suitcase and gym bag. Then the driver said, "I'll get that, young man."

Tony took his sweater, quilted jacket, and camera and headed for the door.

"Anthony?" Mr. Savala said. "The son of my Joseph?"

"Yes, sir. I'm Tony Savala."

"It is good that you arrived without harm," Mr. Savala said. "Come."

He doesn't act very friendly. Maybe he doesn't want me here — any more than I wanted to come. Maybe he thinks I'll be in his way.

This was the first time Tony had thought of how his grandfather might feel about this visit. He'd been concerned about only his own side of the matter, the way *he* felt.

"The truck is parked around the corner," Mr. Savala said. "We'll stow your gear in it. Then go to the hotel to eat. You will soon have your fill of my cooking."

Tony's father had tried to prepare the boy for the kind of meals he'd be eating in the camp wagon. "There'll be no salads, few desserts and a pretty steady diet of scrambled eggs, potatoes, and canned meat.

"But don't turn up your nose, Son," Joe hurried on to say. "You'll be out in the air and be hungry as a bear. Everything'll taste great, especially the Herders' bread."

"What's that?"

"I can't truly tell you what's in it," Joe said. "But it's baked on top of the stove in an iron pot called a Dutch oven. It comes out all crusty and brown. And the cross on the lid forms another on the rounded top. Nothing in my life has ever smelled or tasted better than fresh Herders' bread."

As Tony walked with his grandfather he could think of many things which he'd like to smell right now. Like roses in the backyard at home and the oil on the gears of his Sting Ray bike and the clean wood of a new baseball bat.

4

Ascona Savala walked toward the hotel with steady heavy steps. Tony was surprised that he had to hurry to keep up with his grandfather.

"This must be a funny kind of a hotel," Tony thought. "Will Granddad be the only one in work clothes?" He blinked as he walked into the brightly lighted dining room. Men far outnumbered women and children at the long tables.

"We will eat here. Away from the others," Mr. Savala said.

A waiter, or a man who took their order, came to the table. He didn't look like the waiters Tony'd seen — no uniform or tray or not even a printed menu.

"The usual, Mr. Savala?"

"The usual. That will be fine."

Tony wondered what this usual order was. No one asked him what he wanted.

While they waited for the food five men came over from the next table. They might as well have sat down there in the first place.

Tony understood very few words of the short quick sentences. *It's like Dad said; they speak in Basque a lot of the time.*

Tony looked around the room. He saw a big picture of a mule train on one wall.

Mr. Savala's usual order turned out to be thick steak with slices of silvery onions, rolls, apple pie

23

with cheese, and a boat-shaped dish filled with scoops of ice cream.

The food was good. "But Mom would be upset. No vegetables. Not even potatoes. Maybe that's because the herders have them all the time at camp."

It seemed to Tony that the meal would never end. His grandfather talked more of the time than he ate. He introduced Tony to everyone as the son of his Joseph. Some remembered his father. The strangers looked closely at Tony. One said, "I see the Basque in him."

Tony didn't like that remark, but he didn't say anything — just looked down at his plate. It seemed to him that they sat at the table for hours. Actually it couldn't have been more than forty-five minutes. When they left the hotel the sky was an orangey gold glow in the gap where the road ran west. Purple shadows crept down the mountain slopes.

Ascona led the way to the truck and Tony climbed up the high step. He saw very little on the way out to the sheep camp. For one reason it became dark quickly. The dark seemed to swallow the world in one great gulp. Tony leaned his head against the padded side of the jouncing truck. The motor chugged and rumbled. The air whistled in around the rattling windows. Tony pulled his quilted jacket tight around his neck. His mother had known what she was talking about when she said the nights were cool out in the foothills of the mountains.

Tony dozed off in spite of the cold, noise, and bumping. He didn't get fully awake until the truck came to a jerky stop. He sat up and looked out. All he could see was shadowy shapes of all sizes. There was not one single speck of light anywhere.

"Come, Anthony," Mr. Savala said. "We are at the camp."

They gathered up Tony's gear, deciding to unload the supplies the next day.

Tony felt his way over the uneven ground and around the clumps of bushes trying to keep up with his grandfather.

One of the shadows began to take shape. They were nearing the camp wagon.

Where is the herder who was to watch the flock? Would he go away and leave the sheep?

A sharp barking broke the silence of the night. Then the friendly yelping came closer. Tony could hear the rushing, brushing sound as the dog came through the bushes.

Ascona Savala began to speak in gentle tones but in the Basque language. The shaggy-haired dog jumped up on his owner.

"This is Juniper," Mr. Savala said. "But I almost always call him Junie."

As they came up to the side of the camp wagon Tony saw that there was a faint light coming from the end. As they rounded the side that deep yellow glow was blacked out by a tall figure coming through the door.

"So! You found the lost lamb?" the man said.

"This is Pete Ariat," Mr. Savala said. "Meet the son of my Joseph."

"How do," Pete said. "I can't see you very well. Are you like my old friend Joe?"

"Some people think so," Tony said. He'd long ago

given up trying to understand the way grown-ups looked at kids. His mother's aunt was always saying, "Tony has the Cooper eyes and their cleft chin." Even Tony could see that his chin was like his dad's. Besides, what difference did it make?

"Any trouble, Pete?" Mr. Savala asked.

"No. I caught a peek of that old mountain lion you told me about. Junie took a barking fit and I looked up in time to see the big cat jump off the ledge above a ravine and head up the slope."

"He's got his eye on the lambs," Ascona Savala said. "They'd make him many a tasty meal."

Tony felt a quick throbbing in his throat. Was there real danger here?

"Well, I'll ride on," Pete said. "Tomorrow's another day and I'd better rest up to meet it."

"I'd like to pay you for your time," Mr. Savala said.

"No, no. It was a rest to get away from the noise of the big camp. And it'll be your turn to do me a favor as it has before," Pete said.

Tony heard the snorting of Pete's horse. Then he followed his grandfather into the long narrow camp wagon.

Tony looked around. He saw a small stove and a low cabinet at his left. Two bunk beds ran across the far end. A table and two straight chairs nearly filled the right side. A lamp with a ragged yellow flame hung above the table and threw a circle of light across the middle part of the wagon.

"I'll give a quick look at the flock," Mr. Savala said. "Make yourself at home. Come, Junie."

Tony undressed quickly and climbed into the top

bunk. The night before he'd wondered what kind of noises he'd be hearing at this time. Now he was too tired to listen. He was asleep before his grandfather returned.

5

It took Tony a long time to get awake the next morning. It seemed that he was deep in a soft and peaceful place. A whiff and a sound kept coming into his dreamlike sleep. The smell was a little like home, of something baking in his mother's copper-toned oven. The sound was the sharp barking of a dog.

Finally Tony opened his eyes wide enough to see the rounded top of the camp wagon. The narrow boards had been painted, probably a long time ago. Little flecks of blue still clung to the weather-stained ceiling. He turned over on his side and saw his grandfather set a round iron pot on the small table.

Tony raised up on one elbow. Was this the Herders' bread his father had described? As Tony watched, Ascona Savala took the rounded lid from the pot. The wonderful fragrance of fresh bread filled the wagon. Tony realized that he was hungry.

He swung his legs over the edge of the bunk and reached for his jeans and sweatshirt. The small lumpy pillow fell to the floor.

Mr. Savala turned and said, "So! You are awake. Food is here and the sun is almost up."

"Almost up," Tony thought. "How early is it?"

Tony dressed quickly, glancing at his grandfather now and then. Then he sat down in the straight chair across the table. The seat felt springy. He scooted over enough to see that it was woven of

28

some kind of twine that looked a little like straw.

"You like my chair seat?" Mr. Savala said.

"Sure," Tony answered. "It feels bouncy."

"I make them loose so they spring. There's not room for other chairs. These should rest us."

"You made the seats?" Tony asked.

"Sure thing," Mr. Savala said. "It is something to do on long winter nights."

Tony felt a little more comfortable. *Maybe he does want me here. He's talking more. He's trying.*

"That bread smells great," Tony said. "My dad told me about it — about the cross on top."

"So. My Joseph told you that!" Mr. Savala said. He actually smiled. Then he scooped a fluffy mound of scrambled eggs onto Tony's plate with a heavy tin spoon. "I made tea. I remember your mamma said growing boys don't need coffee."

The mention of his mother reminded Tony that he hadn't unpacked the new gym bag. He jumped up and pulled it down from the end of the bunk. He took out the small radio and other articles so he could get at the plastic box of brownies. He tucked the Bible under the covers on his bunk. He didn't know how his granddad might feel about God and Bibles. No one had ever said anything about religion. How did the Basque think about such things?

Tony set the plastic box of chewy cookies on the end of the table close to the wall. "Mom made these. She said you liked them when you were at our house."

Mr. Savala took a brownie in his hand and began to eat. "The taste is the same as I remember. Like real cream butter and brown sugar. My Joseph's

29

wife has a kind heart."

Suddenly Tony didn't want to talk. A wave of homesickness made him feel choked. The chunks of warm bread went down and they tasted good. But it took some help from the hot tea to get every bite past the lump in his throat.

Mr. Savala rose from the table and said, "It is time to move the flock out to grass. Come. Wear a coat."

Tony grabbed a candy bar and stuffed the transistor radio in his jacket pocket. He hoped there was a station close enough to get some news and music. *Maybe the radio waves can't get over the mountains. Maybe we're cut off from the world.*

Tony started out the door. Then he remembered what his father said about dishes. "Dad washes them once a day. At night. But he wants things neat when he comes in. He's not much to yell, but if I forgot to stack my plate, cup, and silverware in the big blue bowl his voice got pretty loud."

Tony hurried back to the table and gathered up the utensils before he stepped down out of the wagon. The air was crisp and clear. Tony saw the sheep moving several yards ahead. They were like a sea of gray. *Only this sea doesn't roar. It baas.*

The sad sound of the sheep calls were punctuated by Junie's yapping. Tony could see the black and white dog running back and forth, first on one side of the flock then the other.

Ascona Savala was following on foot leading a black horse. A sack was thrown across the saddle. It was filled with something which made bumps.

Tony trotted to catch up. The sheep were moving

faster than he thought. *They're probably hungry.* The flock moved up the slope and then Junie nudged them to turn south. Tony could see that the grass was taller here. Suddenly the dog quit barking and lay down with his head on his front legs. This seemed to be a signal to the sheep. They stopped where they were and began munching and nibbling on the coarse grass. As Tony watched, the flock gradually fanned out over the sloping ground.

"You watch that side," Mr. Savala said. "I'll take the high ground today. Another time we will trade sides."

Tony didn't know what to say. He didn't know what he was supposed to do. He hadn't even thought about doing anything. *Was he supposed to work? On his vacation? Didn't his Granddad get along all right the rest of the time?*

"Keep your eyes open. Lambs stray off. Keep the flock on this side of that ravine."

"Why?" Tony asked. Then he wished he'd been quiet. Mr. Savala's dark eyes flashed and his forehead wrinkled in a frown. Tony had the feeling his grandfather wanted to say "Do it because I say so."

"Sheep are awkward animals. If they get over on their back they can't always get up. If they'd fall in the ravine and land on their back they might die before we found them."

By eleven o'clock Tony was hot, bored, and more homesick than he'd ever been in his life. He didn't look up or out, just in, at his own feelings. He wondered what the kids on Candlewood Hills were doing. And his mother. Was anyone thinking

31

"Keep your eyes open. Lambs stray off."

about him or trying to picture what *he* was doing?

He did wander along the ravine saying, "Shoo," every once in a while to sheep that wandered to the outside. *Was shoo what you said to sheep? Or was that for chickens?*

Tony wished he could find a shady place and sit down. Walking on this rough and sloping ground made his legs feel heavy. He ate the candy bar but was still hungry. What would they do for lunch? His grandfather hadn't said anything about eating at noon.

Tony looked back. He couldn't see the camp wagon. *It's like we're lost, with nothing but sheep, mountains, and sky. And I've got to take this for a whole month. It must have been a lot different for Dad. When he talks about sheepherding he always sounds as if he liked it.*

6

Tony had forgotten to wear his watch. He'd left it hanging above his bed on the wooden peg at the end of the camp wagon. "I guess it's safe," he thought. "Who's around to steal?"

But he wished he knew when and what they were to eat. His stomach said it was noon long before he saw gray smoke curling from the ground on the opposite side of the flock.

Within a half hour Ascona Savala rode his horse around to where Tony was sitting in a nest of coarse grass. "The food is ready. Go eat. While I herd your side."

"OK," Tony said. *He sounds mad. What did I do?*

As Tony started loping to the back of the flock Mr. Savala called, "You can ride Poco, boy."

Tony turned and trotted backward a few steps as he answered, "No, thanks. I'd rather walk." This was true. He'd never ridden a horse although he had wanted to go to a riding class at the stables at the fairgrounds one summer.

I'd still like to learn, but not from Granddad. He'd probably make me feel clumsy and I'd do all the wrong things.

Tony found a can of pork and beans sitting on round stones above the bed of rosy coals of fire. They were bubbling and smelled great. He also saw a tin plate with thick slices of Herders' bread and chunks of deep yellow cheese. A large gray enamelware cup of tea was sitting on a flat stone at the edge of the campfire.

"Well, at least it's not scrambled eggs this time," Tony thought as he began to eat. At first he pictured the table at home with flowers in the middle and his mother's pink flowered dishes. "Maybe there'd be fruit salad, lemon pie, or Salisbury steaks."

Then he realized that what he was eating tasted fine. He didn't remember ever being this hungry before in his whole life.

Tony saw a flicker of yellow in a small aspen tree at the edge of the foothill. "It looks like a canary," he thought. "Could it be a wild one? I wonder what other kinds of birds live out here."

He looked across the flock and saw his grandfather riding a little way down into the ravine. "He's checking on me. Thinks I was careless and let a lamb fall in or stray away."

Many of the sheep were lying down and panting in the midday sun. *I guess they can't eat all day long.* Others were nibbling grass, pulling off bites with quick jerks. And all the time some of the lambs were bleating. "I'll never get used to that sad sound," Tony thought. "I should have brought ear plugs." Then he realized. "I did! There are earphones on my radio. I'll bring them along tomorrow."

The time from that noon to dusk seemed at least twelve hours long. Tony had to fight to keep from going to sleep. He didn't think the rough ground, coarse grass, and bleating of the sheep would keep him from sleeping once he let his eyelids close.

It's so quiet and boring out here. How can I

stand a whole month of this! And only two days are gone — this one not quite.

Before the purple shadows crept past the snow-covered slopes Mr. Savala climbed on Poco and began turning the flock toward the camp.

Tony's legs ached and he was hungry again. He was ready to go to bed by the time his grandfather scrambled eggs and opened a can of peaches. But Ascona Savala said, "We will take turns at washing dishes, too. You do them while I fix Poco's bridle. Tomorrow I will wash."

Tony neither looked up nor answered. He reached for one of his mother's butterscotch brownies. He hadn't expected to have to wash dishes or do anything except stick it out. Why hadn't his father told him about sharing the work?

Mr. Savala carried two buckets of water from the tall tin cans which had been filled at a spring to the west. Tony found soap and cloths on a shelf and did the dishes as nearly like his mother as possible. *Except I'm not using as much water. It doesn't run from a faucet here.*

Mr. Savala didn't talk any more that evening. He took his pipe and sat outside on the steps of the camp wagon. Tony could see the outline of his grandfather's head and smell the tobacco smoke.

After he'd washed his feet in a small round basin Tony dug around in the gym bag until he found the earphones. He plugged them in and lay in his bunk listening to music. It wasn't loud but it was clear.

He turned over and felt the bump his Bible made under the covers. "Mom would like it if I read something every night as we do at home in the mornings. But I'm sleepy. Besides, there's not much light up here."

Tony tried to think of some Bible verses he could say over and over to himself as he floated into sleep. His mother said she often did this especially when she had some problem or worry on her mind. *And I sure do have a problem. How am I going to live through twenty-eight more days of this?*

He tried to think of Bible verses. But all that came to his mind were parts of the Twenty-third Psalm. *The Lord is my shepherd.* How could that make him feel better! Being a shepherd didn't seem like anything very good to Tony. *He maketh me to lie down in green pastures.* Tony and the sheep had been out on green pastures all day. *For the sheep this might be great but not for me.*

Tony was almost asleep when he heard someone calling, "Hey, there, Savala. You awake?"

"Yes. Come on up," Mr. Savala answered.

Within a few minutes Tony recognized the voice. It was Pete Ariat who'd stayed at the camp.

"The boy asleep?" Pete asked.

"It might be," Mr. Savala said. "He was out with the flock all day."

"How's he doing?" Pete asked.

Tony raised his head from his round pillow. Maybe it wasn't right to try to overhear. But he did.

"As good as I expected a city boy. He says little."

I say little. How about him!

"Well, here's why I rode over. Some of the herders who are off Sunday want to come and spend the day with you. Josef says he will cook the achuria he's always talking about."

"What's achuria?" Tony thought.

"The old country dish of milk-fed lamb," Ascona said. "Josef has such a lamb?"

"Yes. In a way. The old man has thinned canned milk for one, feeding since it was weaned from his mother. It's all right if we come?"

"It will be fine," Ascona said. "We can also have music. Anthony might like the company."

"That's what we thought," Pete said. "It must be lonely out here for the boy. We should try to liven things when we see a way."

"Much thanks for coming, Pete. Watch the rocks on the way down the valley."

"Don't worry. My horse has thinking feet."

Tony felt a little better. Pete and the others were trying to be kind. *And Granddad is willing for them to come. Of course, he probably wants company too. He has things to talk about with the other sheepherders, with the real sheepherders. But not with the city son of a Basque.*

7

The next three days were like posts in a row. They followed each other and were the same in almost every way. If there was any difference Tony didn't see it until the middle of Saturday afternoon.

He woke every morning to the sound of pans as his grandfather moved them on the black iron grates of the campstove. And from outside came the always-and-forever baaing of the sheep.

The man and the boy ate without speaking many words. They followed the sheep to grazing places in silence. Mr. Savala spoke only when there was a need and Tony choked back the questions which had begun to come to his mind.

He'd found an egg-shaped rock in a gully on the foothill side of the pasture. It was larger than a hen egg, more like what Tony thought a goose or turkey might lay. It was gray on the outside and rough like most rocks but Tony had the feeling it was something special. He decided to see if Pete Ariat knew anything about it. *He's the only talkative person I've met in this place so far. But then he's the only one — besides Granddad.*

The sun was not far from sinking behind the mountains Saturday afternoon when Tony fell asleep. He'd been leaning against a big boulder and his head fell sidewise. He didn't know how long he'd dozed when a different kind of sound came through the thick fog of sleep.

Tony sat up straight and blinked his eyes. "That's a lamb," he thought. "But this one sounds a little strange. Something's wrong."

He jumped to his feet and glanced quickly toward the other side of the flock. His grandfather was on Poco riding slowly toward the lead sheep. His back was to Tony.

The crying sound was growing fainter. Tony ran slantwise up a small ravine to the left. This led to the upper reaches where the coyotes and mountain lions prowled. *Granddad warned me about them.*

Tony slid on loose rocks as he climbed, but he kept on. He could hear the lost lamb better after he'd gone a few yards. Suddenly he saw the gray woolly coat against the rocks. The little animal was panting from exhaustion. *Maybe he's scared.*

Tony stooped and picked up the lamb with his arms, cradling it from underneath and the long legs dangling. He'd seen how his grandfather carried the little ones.

The stray was back with the flock before Ascona Savala turned Poco and headed back Tony's way. "He probably didn't see what's been happening," Tony thought. "Should I tell him? Wouldn't he be mad? And after all it came out all right. The lamb's OK."

Tony kept his eyes wide open the rest of the afternoon. This wasn't too hard to do because they took the herd in early.

Mr. Savala rode around and said, "We will go now. The wagon needs cleaning before tomorrow and Isidoro will be coming to take the laundry to Winnemucca."

He'd seen how his grandfather carried the little ones.

Tony was told to take all the bedclothing out into the sun to air. "Spread it on the bushes," Mr. Savala said. "Then carry the chairs and boots outside, so I can scrub the floor."

Isidoro came by in a rattling Jeep and stopped along the road above them. He whistled as he came to the camp wagon.

"You are happy," Ascona said grinning at the slim black-haired young man.

"Why would I not be? It's Saturday, I have my pay, and there's a Basque girl who works at the bakeshop who smiles at me."

"Then you will not hate to make a trip to that shop. I need three of the berry pies for tomorrow. You know some friends from the camp are coming?"

"I know!" Isidoro said. "It is my bad luck that I must work."

"Then use the change to get yourself something," Ascona said. "And set the pies inside the door."

After Isidoro left with the canvas sack of clothes bouncing on his back Tony found enough courage to ask, "Don't you ever lock the door?"

Mr. Savala said, "Why should it be locked?"

"Well, to keep someone from stealing stuff," Tony said.

"There is no one out here but Basque. It is a tradition that Basque do not steal. Now we must carry in the covers before the night dew falls."

The camp wagon looked neat and smelled clean. Mr. Savala opened Vienna sausages and mixed canned fruit to go with the crusty fried potatoes.

Before he picked up his bone-handled fork Mr. Savala pulled his black leather billfold out of his shirt pocket. He took out a five-dollar bill and gave it to Tony.

"What's this for?"

"For working."

"But I didn't expect to get paid. And I didn't do much."

"You didn't expect to have to work either," Mr. Savala said looking straight at his grandson. "When you do more you'll be paid more."

Tony said, "Thank you, sir," and ducked his head. His face felt hot. *He knows I expected to play around and that I didn't like being told what to do. He may not say much but he knows plenty. Is that partly why Dad wanted me to know his father?*

Tony decided to write to his parents. He realized that if he'd written the night before, Isidoro could have mailed the letter that night. But he thought that his grandfather said someone from the big camp went in to town on Mondays for supplies. *I can have them mail this.*

Tony wrote until his hand ached. He said more about the fact that people were coming to visit them than anything else. Nothing else seemed exciting. He did tell about the egg-shaped rock and the yellow bird which looked like a canary. After he signed the letter he wrote, "You're right, Dad. The Herders' bread is great — especially when it's warm."

He decided to read awhile and sort through the half-dozen paperbacks his mother had chosen. Two were Danny Orlis books, but he wasn't in the mood for mystery or suspense. Not tonight. Then he saw the title *Get Smart* and leafed through the pages. It was about the Proverbs and had a lot of pictures showing how they were related to life. "This is great," he thought. "I'm going to take it out on the range someday."

By this time he felt as if he had to prop his eyelids open. But he just couldn't get to sleep. He thumped his pillow on both sides and turned over three times.

Then he faced the truth. He knew why he was still awake. There was something on his mind.

He raised up on one elbow. His grandfather was shaving, brushing foamy soapsuds into his salt-and-pepper whiskers.

"Grandfather, I didn't tell you. But a lamb strayed toward the mountains this afternoon."

Mr. Savala didn't hesitate in stroking his beard with the ivory-handled brush.

"So?" he said.

"I heard it and followed the cry," Tony explained.

"Did you drive it back?"

"No, sir. I carried it — like you do."

Mr. Savala kept right on shaving, pulling the long sharp blade down over his left cheek. Tony could hear the scraping sound. *Is he going to bawl me out? Or not talk at all?*

Mr. Savala turned and looked up at Tony. "Maybe I paid you too soon. Could be you deserve another dollar."

8

The camp wagon was a quiet place when Tony opened his eyes the next morning. He listened and could hear the bleating of sheep, but it was faint and far away. Where were they? Had Grandfather started toward the grazing range? Then Tony remembered it was Sunday. Ascona Savala had said he saved the land above the camp near a thick aspen grove for Sunday feeding. "We can sit on the steps and watch them — with Junie's help."

Tony locked his hands behind his head and stared at the ceiling but his thoughts were back in Indianapolis. He didn't know what time it was there, but felt it wouldn't be long before his parents would be walking across the alley then over to the church.

He wondered if the iris roots were growing and if the new choir robes had arrived. *And what will Mom have for Sunday dinner. Fried chicken?*

Tony felt a little homesick, but his throat didn't feel as tight and choky as it did at first. *That might be on account of company coming. Something different is going to happen today.*

He decided to get up and dress, being careful to hang his clothes on the pegs. Then he smoothed the covers of his bed, trying to make it look as neat as the lower bunk.

A red and white checked towel covered something on the table. He peeked and saw a piece of berry pie on a tin plate. There was also a fresh loaf of Herders' bread. His granddad must have been up a long time. Tony found a note printed on a piece of brown wrapping paper. "Eat. Wash up and come out."

As Tony stepped out of the wagon he heard a tinkling, a bell sound. Then he saw three strange horses tied to the short hitching rail. "The men from the other camp are already here." Tony shaded his eyes and looked up. He saw his grandfather and the others heading back from the head of the flock.

One was Pete Ariat. Tony was glad. The other two were near the age of his grandfather. They were square shouldered and the hair of one was as white as the wool his mother was using to knit a sweater.

Pete walked a little ahead of the others. When he came near Tony he said, "Listen to them. Put three old country Basque together and you'd think they'd never left the Pyrenees."

"Can you understand what they're saying?" Tony asked.

"Sure. I've grown up with it. Heard little else till I went to school. You don't know what they're saying?"

Tony shook his head. "No, my dad taught me a few words." Then he nodded toward the other men. "But I don't hear any of those words in what they're saying."

"Well, they're talking about the bell that Julio brought for your granddad's lead sheep. His was lost a while back."

"I thought I heard a bell," Tony said. "What good does it do?"

"It helps keep sheep from straying. They stay closer to the leader," Pete said.

When the three older men came up to Tony, Ascona Savala said, "My friends, this is Anthony, the son of my Joseph. Say greetings to Josef and Julio."

Tony surprised himself by walking up and shaking hands with his grandfather's friends. He knew his parents would have expected him to be that polite. But before now he hadn't really been glad to meet anyone out here.

Josef looked up at the sun, squinting his brown eyes and arching the bushy brows. "The day is getting older. I should start the achuria."

"I'll bring the lamb," Pete said grinning. "He had me up until one o'clock dressing the little one in the cool of the night."

Tony wasn't too excited about this Basque dish. His mother almost never cooked lamb. *But I guess I can try it.*

He watched as his grandfather raked ashes from the bed of coals. Evidently Ascona Savala had built the fire very early.

"Say, Tony," Pete said, "we will only be in the way here. These cooks would not let us spoil their achuria. Want to go rock hunting up the slopes?"

"Rock *hunting?*" Tony said. "You don't have to hunt them around here."

"Certain kinds you do," Pete said. "I have a hunch that there's pink quartz up there someplace."

"Sure, I'll go," Tony said. "But first I want

to ask you about a funny one I found."

He hurried into the camp wagon and brought out the egg-shaped stone.

Pete took it and held it on the palm of his hand. "This is a thunder egg," he said.

"A thunder egg," Tony said. "Why would a rock have a name like that?"

"Search me!" Pete said. "If there's a good reason I never did hear it."

Tony knew right then that he was going to find out when he got home. He'd look in the encyclopedia or ask a science teacher or something.

"Is this rock special in some way?"

"It sure is," Pete said. "Let's see if Ascona has a sharp chisel or hatchet and a hammer. And I'll show you. That is I will if you want this egg cracked open. It's yours."

"Well, go ahead," Tony said. "If the special part's inside, I want to see. Granddad's toolbox is under his bed."

Tony watched as Pete worked to anchor the thunder egg and felt its surface. "I have to find the center," he said. "Or else it won't split clean."

With a hard sharp blow the stone egg fell into two even sections. Tony gasped as he picked up one half. "It's blue and gold inside and a little silvery in places."

"Then turn it around and look at it from all angles," Pete said. "A lot of times you'll see a picture. One of mine shows a side view of a man who looks a lot like Abraham Lincoln."

"Really?" Tony said. Then he looked carefully at his own stone. "Hey, Pete! It's a sunset. See it."

"Sure is," Pete said. "And that dark blue is like mountains. The East Humboldt range maybe."

"How did the color and design get inside this rough gray stone?" Tony asked.

"Search me," Pete said.

"Well, thanks for showing me," Tony said. "You ready to go up the slope? I'd like to see that pink quartz you were talking about."

The tall young man who'd always lived near the Sierra Nevadas and the boy from central Indiana scrambled farther up the slopes than Tony had been. Tony looked back every few minutes. The camp seemed to move farther and farther away and the camp wagon grew smaller.

Pete kept looking at the ground and he saw other things besides rock specimens. Tony wouldn't have even noticed much of what Pete found. "Deer have been here this morning," Pete said. "See the tracks." Once the dark-haired young man jerked his head backward and looked up toward the high peaks. "The coyotes are after something over beyond the rim. Be fine with me if they stay over there."

9

The sun was directly over the camp when Josef said the achuria was ready to eat. The smell of the roasting lamb was tempting to Tony. This surprised him.

Ascona Savala unhinged the back door of the camp wagon and laid it on two big rocks. It teetered a little, but not much. He spread the door with newspapers and had Tony bring out tin plates, the bone-handled silverware and enamel cups.

"We will eat under the blue sky where there is room to stretch out afterward."

Tony wondered what he meant by stretching out. Were they all going to take a nap? Sometimes his parents did that on Sunday afternoon. *And I hate that way of spending Sunday. It's a big old waste.*

Ascona had made a bowl of potato salad while Pete and Tony were rock hunting. It was still eggs and potatoes but they were put together with dressing; tasting *something* like what his mother used.

Pete carried out the berry pies and Julio had made the coffee. Just as they were starting to fill their plates Mr. Savala said, "The tea. I did not make tea for Tony."

"That's the first time he's called me that," Tony thought. "I've always been Anthony or the son of his Joseph."

"Don't bother, Grandfather," Tony said. "I'll drink water or put lots of canned milk in some coffee."

50

Whatever Josef put in the achuria had changed the lamb taste into something spicy and a little sweet. None of the men said much during the meal. And afterwards no one made a move to put away food or wash dishes. Mr. Savala threw three towels over the food and then stretched out on the grass.

"Here it comes," Pete whispered to Tony. "The storytelling."

"Stories?"

"Yes. Tales of the old days back in the land of the Basque."

"I probably won't know what they're talking about," Tony said.

"I will translate for you," Pete said. "I could ask them to speak in English. But they did not go to school in this country. Their stories lose much meaning when they don't tell them in the speech of their homeland."

"You said *their* homeland," Tony said. "You don't call it yours?"

Pete shook his head. "No, I don't. It's in their memory, not mine."

"I guess that's the way it is for my dad," Tony said.

The storytelling began. It was a little like a play. Each man told certain parts as if it was rehearsed. *That's probably because they've done this over and over.*

"Some of the things they're saying wouldn't interest you," Pete said, "and I've already heard it too many times. But there's one story that I'll never be tired of hearing. Take a snooze and before they come to it I'll wake you."

"What's it about?" Tony asked.

"The doves," Pete said.

Tony wondered what could be interesting about doves but he saw that Pete was listening to what Julio was saying. So he asked no questions. Not then.

Tony curled up, resting his head on one arm and throwing the other across his eyes. He could hear the wild canaries chirping in the aspen grove. The tinkling of the bell on the lead sheep and the bleating of lambs came from the flock. When he opened his eyes he could see the little hairs on his arms glinting like gold in the sun.

He didn't really go to sleep, just stayed in a place in between. He could hear the murmur of voices, smell the tobacco smoke and feel the scratchy grass on his cheek.

Suddenly Pete said, "Wake up, Tony. They've finished the dove story. Now comes the singing."

Tony looked across at the three old friends. They sat against boulders and had a faraway look in their eyes. Julio led out in the saddest sounding music Tony had ever heard. It was like crying and pain and homesickness all mixed together. Even if the words were Basque the music sent a message to Tony.

When the song ended the three men poured coffee from the tall pot and looked away into the west as they sipped.

Pete motioned for Tony to follow him to the edge of the aspen trees.

"First, let me tell you the words of the song," Pete said as they found a cool place to sit. "It goes something like this:

'White dove, white dove,
Tell me if you please
Where were you traveling,
Your route so straight, your heart at ease.

'From my country
I departed with the thought of seeing Spain.
I flew as far as the Pyrenees,
There lost my pleasure
And found pain.'°

"That's not exactly right," Pete said. "It gets changed when it's translated.

"I've heard that song all my life," Pete said. "By now the dove's the same as the Basque. People don't really know where we come from, and we do a lot of going from place to place. But the dove song came from something that seems cruel to me."

"Cruel?" Tony said. "How — what?"

"Well, this goes on even today. The dove hunts. There's a thing called a palombierre. It's really a dove hunt — or a slaughter.

"Big nets are strung across a mountain pass. Men are stationed in a hut in a great big tree. When doves come through the pass and are close enough so the men in the hut can hear the drumming of their wings the men throw wooden clubs from the hut. The birds dive down right into the nets and are trapped."

"But why?" Tony asked.

"They eat them," Pete said. "Some of them right then. Others are penned for eating later."

°Dove Song from "The Land of Ancient Basques," Robert Laxalt, *National Geographic*, Vol. 134: No. 2: Aug.: p. 243.

"It doesn't seem fair," Tony said.

"I know," Peter answered. "My cousin went to see a palombierre when he was in the old country. He said he felt sick. It took him a long time to get to sleep for several nights. He kept seeing the exploding of feathers when the doves hit the nets. And he said he wanted to climb up and unfasten the birds from the webs."

"Why do the men keep telling things like this?" Tony asked. "It didn't make them look happy."

"I suppose it's part of their hold on the homeland," Pete said. "It's a custom, an old way. You see, Tony, the Basques have been a people who wanted to keep to themselves, holding on to customs. Even their stories help them feel a part of the race. But this part is in a faraway place."

"Will you always be a sheepherder, Pete?" Tony asked.

"I doubt it," Pete said. "The big owners are taking over. I don't like working for others. I'm saving my pay to buy a small ranch like your grandfather did."

Tony knew that Ascona Savala owned land outside Winnemucca. He was about to ask Pete why his grandfather didn't live there when Julio called to them.

"Come. There is more food to eat before the day ends."

10

Ascona Savala stirred up the coals of the fire, added wood and made a fresh pot of coffee. Then he uncovered the leftovers. "Eat before you go back to camp," he said. "The cook will not have anything as good as this. And the lamb is yours."

As they chose food to put on their plates, Pete said, "Listen, old ones. If you tell any more tales of the Basques land, speak English. Tony here has had enough of my translating. And my throat is tired, from keeping up with you."

"So?" Julio said. "Who would ever believe that Pete Ariat would become weary of talking? That day we will never see!"

Ascona Savala turned to look at Tony. "Is there something you'd like to hear? Or have you had enough of the tales of the homeland?"

Tony didn't know what to say. He would have just as soon talked about baseball, astronauts, or something American and up to date. But some questions *had* come to his mind during this day and the week before. *Maybe I'd better ask them now. Granddad talks more when other Basques are around.*

"Well," Tony said as he cut off a bite of berry pie. "I heard Pete say something about a Basque Festival. Is this like a state fair or a rodeo maybe? And is it in France or Spain?"

"The one Pete spoke of is here. It is held each August in Elko," Mr. Savala said. "It is for Basques but other sheepherders go, and the tourists too."

"It *is* a little like a fair," Pete said.

"How could you know that?" Julio asked. "Have you been to one of these state fairs?"

"I have," Pete said. "I am not tied to this canyon like you. I was in the bluegrass section of Kentucky. That was the year I went with Mr. Cordell to buy rams. Remember that?"

"We could not forget. You tell it often," Ascona said. "But you never spoke of any fair. How is it like our festival?"

"Only in one main way, I guess," Pete said. "Many people come to see what goes on. In Kentucky they see horse shows, livestock, and many other things. In Elko we get together for dancing, strength contests, and singing."

"Who looks after the sheep while people go to Elko?" Tony asked.

"It is always the same," Julio said. "We go by turns."

"And we must go now," Pete said. "Your horses are not as sure-footed as mine. The sky is cloudy and the moon will not give us much light."

Tony hated to see the visitors leave for two reasons. The day had been like a long recess from loneliness. And he knew the stack of dishes and tableware would have to be washed. *It's my turn. That's my clunky luck.*

Ascona told Tony to start carrying things back into the camp wagon. "I will put the door on the wagon and help Junie bring the sheep down closer to camp."

Tony shook his head and screwed his face up in

disgust as he looked at the pile of dishes to be washed. *It'll take me an hour to do all these.*

He heard the bolt drop in the hinge of the door. Then his grandfather stopped on the steps long enough to say, "Put two kettles of water on. I'll give you a hand with that stack."

Mr. Savala didn't say a word while they washed dishes. Tony glanced sidewise at times to see if his grandfather looked mad or sick.

I guess he's tired of talking. No wonder! His tongue has had a real workout today.

Tony decided to read awhile. He turned up the wick of the kerosene lamp and tried to get comfortable on one of the straight chairs. He thought of the soft couch and deep chairs at home. Within a few minutes he decided the book wasn't interesting enough to make up for sitting up so straight.

He got ready for bed and lay with the earphones plugged into his radio. He drifted off to sleep then gave a frightening jerk. After that he couldn't get back to sleep because of the pictures that rolled before his eyes like a film which never stopped. He kept seeing helpless doves trapped in webbed nets.

Tony looked over the edge of the bunk. His grandfather was rubbing some kind of grease into his heavy work shoes. Mr. Savala's motions were so strong that his partly gray hair bounced with each stroke.

"He needs a haircut," Tony thought. "Maybe we will get to go to town for that. But then who'd look after the sheep while we were away, Little Boy Blue?"

The remaining three weeks of Tony's summer as a shepherd stretched before him like a road which had no end.

Tomorrow I'll go back to baby-sitting with the lambs.

He closed his eyes and again he saw the fluttering of the wings of birds. Tony wondered if his dad had heard this story. *Probably. Pete said it was the one tale Basque never failed to tell.*

"I don't understand Dad sometimes," Tony thought. "He wants me to learn about my origins. What's so great about having ancestors who trap wild birds in hidden nets?"

Suddenly Tony had to know something. It seemed important. He raised up so straight he bumped his head on the blue-flecked ceiling.

"Grandfather," he said. "Did you ever trap doves? When you lived in the homeland I mean? Or here either?"

Mr. Savala peered into the gloominess of the end of the camp wagon.

"No, I saw it once. The palombierre was not far from the home of my grandmother. But I was only a boy. And my father brought me to this land before many months went by. This was after my mother's last sickness."

"But you never trapped them?"

"No." Then Mr. Savala rose and stood within a yard of the bunks. "Is there a reason why you ask?"

"Yes, I guess so. You see, it seems a cruel thing to me."

"And you did not want to think you were left

alone with a mean old Basque?"

"That sounds pretty bad," Tony thought. "But he's partly right."

Mr. Savala sat down again and kneaded the back of his neck with his strong brown hand. "It was cruel. It is," he said. "I am happy that there's never been a need to bring the custom of the palombierre to this land."

"No need?" Tony asked.

"There is more food here," Ascona said. "Even in the bad times we did not need to trick the wide-winged birds into being our meals."

Tony lay back on the bed. This time he didn't see beating, fluttering wings. The only picture that flashed into his mind was of his grandfather greasing his work shoes.

Tony floated off to sleep with the words, "He anointeth my head with oil." *This shepherd life must be getting to me.*

11

The whinny of one of the horses called to Tony in his sleep. At first the sound seemed to be part of a dream. It seemed Tony was at a rodeo and someone whose face was unfamiliar was coaxing Tony to ride a pawing brown and white horse.

Then a groan caused Tony to open his eyes. He slid out of his bunk and looked in the lower bed. No one was there. Tony ran his hand over the covers to be sure.

Then he heard a noise at the door. "Anthony," his grandfather was saying. "Are you up?"

Tony bumped into the chair he'd left pulled out from the table and stumbled over something. *Maybe I should have found the matches and lit the lamp.* His heart was thumping in his throat as he opened the wooden door.

Mr. Savala was sitting on the lowest step. There was enough light from the moon for Tony to see that his grandfather's right leg was stretched out straight.

"What's the matter?" Tony asked. "What's been going on?"

"There was something wrong with the flock," Ascona said. His breath seemed to be coming in jerks.

"I mean what happened to you?" Tony asked.

"I hurried out to see about the sheep. Did not take time to put the laces back in my shoes.

"What's the matter?" Tony asked.

Then when I went up the slope to the east my foot slipped. The ankle twisted."

"Do you suppose it's broken?" Tony asked.

"No, no. I can feel that no bones are sticking out."

Tony was relieved. His thoughts had raced like a movie projector at high speed. He'd pictured himself riding through the night for help to somewhere — Winnemucca maybe or to the big camp wherever it was. And mountain lions, coyotes, and snakes appeared in the flashing scenes in Tony's mind.

"Don't you think we should take off your shoe?" Tony asked. "Sprained ankles swell. I had one once."

"This is true," Mr. Savala said. "The swelling has started. It began when I went on to the night pasture."

"You went on up?" Tony asked.

"I am a shepherd," Ascona Savala said quietly. "There was a noise in the flock. Danger seemed near."

"What was it? Do you know?" Tony asked.

"A coyote. I heard its barking go farther away."

"Do you want me to try to take your shoe off?" Tony said.

"You can try. When I leaned over a short time ago the strain and pain made me cry out," Mr. Savala said.

Tony wished he was someplace else. He was scared and didn't know what was coming next. *But I'm the only one here to do this. Who else can help?*

So he knelt down facing his grandfather and took the shoe by both hands. He began to work gently tugging — first at the heel, then the toe. "It's a tight fit," he said. "But it's giving. It's a good thing now that the shoestrings aren't in."

Tony knew that his grandfather must be in pain. But he didn't give a sign.

When the foot was free, Tony squeezed back around the injured man and went in the wagon to light the lamp. As he waited for the oil-soaked wick to sputter into a golden flame he wondered what he should do next. *Should I heat water? Or is it cold that's good for sprains? But we don't have any ice.*

He turned to see his grandfather coming through the door. The light was good enough for Tony to see that the man's usually brown face was white around the mouth and nose. Big beads of moisture had appeared on his forehead.

Tony quickly scooted a chair over closer to the door.

"Do you think you should soak it or something?" Tony asked.

"No, no. I'll hobble over to the bunk in a little bit. Then you can prop it up with something."

"I know what would be good," Tony said. "My sleeping bag. It's springy and soft."

"Fine," Mr. Savala said. He strained a little as he reached down to take off the other shoe but didn't cry out.

"Do you have aspirin or anything for the pain?" Tony asked.

"For the pain?" Mr. Savala said. "I never take anything. But I've not had much hurting like this. Only the kind that comes when a loved one suffers or leaves." Then he raised his dark eyes and looked quickly at Tony. "Like your grandmother's going."

"But he meant Dad too," Tony thought. "I know he did. Dad's leaving gave him pain."

Mr. Savala held on to the table, chair, and wall as he limped to the end of the wagon.

He sank down and Tony raised the injured foot and propped it up with the roll of quilted sleeping bag.

"You make a good nurse for a boy," Mr. Savala said as he wiped his forehead with a red handkerchief.

"Well, I'm just doing stuff my Mom does for me." *I sure wish she was here.* "Is there anything else I could do?"

Mr. Savala looked down at the swollen foot. "There is a bottle of liniment in the tin box under this bunk. Some say it takes away swelling."

Tony found the tall flat-sided bottle and pried out the cork with the tine of a fork.

"Whew!" he said. "That stuff smells strong, and awful."

Mr. Savala smiled. "It does. Julio gave me the liniment. He says it will cure anything. But I tell him the smell's so bad you forget about the pain."

"You want me to try it?" Tony asked.

"Go ahead. It's here. Then you'd better sleep a little longer. There will be much to do tomorrow."

"Can you sleep?" Tony asked later as he tried to wash the smell of the liniment from his hands.

"I may not," Mr. Savala said. "But I can rest and keep quiet."

Tony did go back to sleep but not for several minutes. He thought about the coming day. *What will we do? Will I have to take the flock up to pasture by myself? Or will Grandfather send me to get help?*

Then he wondered, "What would he do if I weren't here? It could happen. No one comes down from the main road for days at a time. A lot of bad things have time to happen."

He knew from his father that Ascona Savala wanted to keep his own flock, to work for himself. Joe often told Tony, "My father's as independent as they come. That's why he won't sell out and work for the big companies. In a way I understand this. But a lone sheepherder has problems."

Tony had begun to think he'd never get back to sleep when he remembered about the laundry and the mail. Someone was to come by on the way to Winnemucca the next morning.

His mind was relieved enough so that he heard nothing until his grandfather called. "Anthony! Can you come to the door before whoever's out there pounds it into splinters?"

"It's me, Mr. Savala," someone said. "Isidoro. What's wrong that your sheep are in the pen when the sun is above the east gap?"

12

Tony jerked on his last clean pair of jeans as he hurried to the door. "Why didn't you come on in?" he said to Isidoro. "You know the Basque don't lock doors."

"That is the truth," the young sheepherder said. "But there are other things we do not do. Like walking into a man's home without being invited."

"So you're invited — and welcome," Tony said.

"What's this!" Isidoro said in surprise. "Ascona Savala not up. Is the world still turning?"

"He's hurt," Tony said. "It's his ankle."

"Yes, the boy is right," Mr. Savala said, rising up on one elbow. "The sureness of foot left me last night when a coyote came near the night pen."

Isidoro walked over and looked at the swollen ankle. The skin was a mixture of purple and yellow. "That's a bad sprain. You need to go to the doctor in Winnemucca."

"This is what I'd thought," Mr. Savala said. "But there are the sheep."

Isidoro looked at Tony, who could almost read his mind. *He's thinking a Basque boy my age would take the flock to pasture without hesitating even long enough to bat an eye.*

Tony found himself saying, "I can take the sheep out. Junie will help. You can go into town with Isidoro."

Mr. Savala began to shake his head. "The day

would be too long. It takes until the middle of the afternoon to get supplies loaded and laundry done. I'd not want to be gone that long."

"He means he doesn't trust me with the sheep all day," Tony thought. "And I don't even trust myself."

Isidoro reached up to set his tan felt hat on the back of his head. Tony didn't know why but he'd wished a few times lately that he had a hat like the other Basques wore. He'd want his to have a brim that rolled at the sides as tightly as Pete Ariat's, and a headband of red and gold.

"I tell you what!" Isidoro said. "Pete Ariat and his brother are at this end of our range. While you get ready I'll go back and see if Pete can get someone to take his place. Then he can ride over to stay with Tony."

"Who'd he get?" Tony asked.

"The boss took on a couple of college kids a week back. They're what you might call roustabouts — fill in here and there. Pete or his brother Paul Ariat, could teach them more about sheep than they know now in half an hour," Isidoro said.

"I don't like putting people out of their way," Ascona Savala said. "But this does seem a fine plan."

Tony followed Isidoro outside. "Thanks a lot," he said. "Junie and I'll take the flock on out. Listen to them bleat!"

"They're hungry," Isidoro said. "Which way you going? So I can tell Pete."

"Back toward the west and beyond that grove up there. See it?"

"I see. Take care, boy. Don't let that old mountain

lion slip up on you."

Tony grinned and waved, but he wished Isidoro hadn't mentioned the wild animal. *That's not much help.*

He hurried back into the wagon. "Can I fix you something to eat?" he asked Mr. Savala.

"Nothing cooked. Open a can of meat. There's bread enough. You can take the rest of your mother's good cakes. Pete may not be here by noon."

Tony brought in a pitcher of water and set it and a cup on a chair near the bunk. Then he fixed cold food for both. "I'll put mine in this plastic box and eat out there. The sheep are about to butt down the fence to get at grass."

"Don't you want to ride Trotter or the pack pony?"

Tony didn't want to even take a horse. He'd slipped out a time or two in the evening and climbed on the poky fat pony. He still didn't feel easy about being on a horse, especially out here where a runaway could go so far. There were no fences to stop its flight.

Then he thought, "But I'd better take one horse. If something went wrong on one side of the flock I couldn't get over there very fast."

"I'll take Poco," he said, "if that's OK?"

"Sure thing," Mr. Savala said. "Move quiet like. Don't frighten the sheep into running and you'll get along fine."

"I won't scare them," Tony thought. "I just hope the coyotes and mountain lions stay up on the high slopes."

"See you," Tony said and hurried toward the

pen. Junie was waiting at the gate. The dog turned and made a quick dash back toward the camp wagon. "Come, Junie," Tony said. This is how his granddad called the shaggy dog to work.

When the sheep surged out the wide gate Junie's instincts took over. He circled and darted, nudging the swiftly moving flock toward the grazing area. Tony had to trot to keep up, jerking on Poco's bridle so the pony would keep up. He almost dropped his box of lunch.

I might as well ride. Maybe I can make her speed up by digging at her with my heels. She's about to jerk my arms out of the sockets.

Riding didn't seem so bad by the time the sheep reached the tall grass. Tony realized he could see more from the pony's back. The stragglers and strays showed up sooner. *Maybe Poco's legs will save mine.*

The sheep were so hungry that they did little moving once they'd reached food. Tony had time to sit in the shade of a tree and eat. He tried not to look back toward the camp. He was out of sight of the wagon and couldn't see when Isidoro came back for his grandfather. Tony knew Pete would ride in from that direction, and he'd sure be glad to see him.

Tony had left in such a hurry and flurry that he'd forgotten to bring either his watch or radio. As the sun rose higher he thought, "This way I've got a lot of time to think, but I don't know how much."

All kinds of questions ran through his mind. *What if his grandfather had to go to the hospital? What would happen to the sheep? Or to me?*

Should he have slipped out and written a note to

his dad about the ankle? Was it that serious?

Tony climbed on Poco when the sun was almost above his head. He'd decided to ride around and see if any lamb had fallen into a ravine or was lost in the brush. *Besides, maybe I can see Pete sooner.*

He'd circled the slowly moving flock when he heard someone calling. He raised up and saw Pete riding around a pile of boulders. Tony waved and waited. He wanted to ride to meet him, but knew he shouldn't leave.

"Hi, boy," Pete said as he rode up. "What's happened? Is there another Basque shepherd in this canyon?"

Tony smiled. He knew he'd never want to come out here and live. But strange as it seemed to him he didn't feel uneasy about being called a shepherd. It was only for the summer.

"Man, I'm glad to see you," Tony said.

"Getting hungry are you?" Pete said. "Well, I begged some stew and corn bread from our cook. Let's eat."

"This is good," Tony said later. "And it's not scrambled eggs or beans. Say, Pete! Where does Grandfather get all the eggs we eat? I've not seen one chicken since I've been here."

Pete grinned. "They're powdered eggs," he said.

"I thought they tasted different from what we have at home," Tony said.

"That's why we mix potatoes and eggs most of the time," Pete said. "To muffle the powdered taste."

"Did you have any trouble getting time off to come here?" Tony asked as he munched on the moist corn bread.

"Nope," Pete answered. "I've had some time coming to me. I worked during shearing time for a guy whose wife was sick. I'm going to stay here until Ascona gets back on two feet."

"That's a relief!" Tony said.

13

The rest of the day was almost like the others
Tony had spent on the range. He kept watch
over one side of the flock while Pete patrolled
the other. The sun was hot and the sheep moved,
ate, and bleated as usual. There was no one close
enough so Tony could talk.

Yet there was a difference. *Things seem a lot
better than they did an hour ago. I'm not out here
alone. And a way worked out to get Grandfather to
the hospital. I'm still here and Indianapolis is just
as far away. Do worse times make bad things seem
better?*

The sun was almost touching the highest peaks
when Pete began to turn the flock toward camp.
Junie barked and wagged his tail as they came
within sight of the wagon. The dog had seen
Ascona Savala sitting outside.

Pete had also seen his old friend. "Well, they
let him come home," he said to Tony who was
riding alongside.

"I saw," Tony said. "But where'd that chair
come from? And what's that leaning on the arm?"

"It's a crutch," Pete said. "He went away with one
good leg. Now he has an extra. It's a good thing I
fixed it so I can stay awhile. I've heard of shepherds with a crook, but not with a crutch."

Ascona Savala was scratching Junie's head as Pete
and Tony slid from the horses.

"Well, did they decide you were worth patching up?" Pete asked.

"I made that decision," Mr. Savala said. "They only had to agree with me."

"It wasn't broken was it?" Tony asked.

"No, no. Only a sprain. The doctor said for me to stay off it for a week. But they don't know Ascona Savala. I can be at work in a day or two."

"I'll not argue with you," Pete said. "That's a waste of time. We'll wait and see."

"Pete's staying to help," Tony said. "So rest while he's here anyway. Say — where'd you get that chair?"

"I bought it in town. If I have to sit around it would be better to sit easy. Look, this back will go back on the notches."

"I know," Tony said. "We have some at home just like it. They fold up."

"You like this kind of chair?" Mr. Savala asked.

"Sure."

"Then look at the side of the wagon. There are two more. We don't always have to sit on the grass when friends come."

"Getting kind of reckless with your money aren't you?" Pete said.

"Is it reckless to spend for loved ones and good friends?" Ascona said.

"Who's going to be cook tonight?" Pete asked.

"Let's both of us do it," Tony said.

"There is a box of food on the table," Mr. Savala said. "And a real chocolate cake from the bakery."

As Tony started up the steps his grandfather said, "Wait, Anthony! I forgot. There are letters and a package from your home on your bed."

"Great!" Tony said.

"You go ahead, Tony," Pete said, "I'll try to find a place to put this stuff while you read your mail."

"Don't bother to put that cake away," Tony said. "I have a place to put a big chunk of it."

Tony hesitated. Which should he open first, the letters or the package? That pause didn't last more than two seconds. He ripped open both letters and hurriedly skimmed through them. *I'll read them over after supper.*

Tony was lost in the news from home for nearly ten minutes. Everyone was well. The Carvers had started to build a swimming pool in the backyard. His mother was teaching five-year-olds in the daily Vacation Bible School. Tony's Little League team had won four out of seven games so far.

At the end of the second letter Mrs. Savala wrote, "We may have a surprise for you before another week is over. Your father went to Greenwood tonight to do some more looking. And he has some arrangements to make about getting time off from his work. It wouldn't be right for me to tell you and get your hopes all built up and then have the whole thing fall flat."

"How about my curiosity?" Tony thought. "What could they be doing? Building a pool — no, I don't think so. Dad wouldn't help with it. He's not handy with tools."

Tony tore open the package. It held new flashlight batteries, a box of his mother's caramels, and two more paperbacks.

"Here, Pete," Tony said, "would one of these spoil

your appetite? Mom makes them."

"Nothing that small could fill the cave of my hunger," Pete said. "How about your peeling some potatoes while I ask Ascona how to cook these wieners?"

"Oh, boy. Hot dogs!" Tony said. "Did he buy any buns?"

"He did. And mustard and catsup."

The evening was full of good feeling. Pete teased Mr. Savala and made him smile several times. After the dishes were washed they went back outside and sat in the canvas and metal chairs.

The sheep were quieter than usual. The bleating was soft. Junie lay at Mr. Savala's feet with his head on his paws. Sometimes he wagged the plume of his tail. The jays and wild canaries in the aspen grove sang a nightsong.

"Say, it nearly slipped out of my mind," Mr. Savala said. "I saw the insurance man in town. He said the people who've lived in my house are moving out in a month."

"Are you going to have him look for another renter?" Pete asked. "Or are you using your brains?"

"I told him to let the thing rest for awhile," Mr. Savala said. "I been turning your words over in my mind. I will take some of this sitting time to write to Joseph about the matter."

"They sent you messages, Grandfather," Tony said. "When we go in you can read the letters yourself."

Pete stretched and yawned. Tony found himself doing the same. "Where are you going to sleep, Pete?"

"Under the stars," Pete said. "I brought my bedroll."

Tony thought of his sleeping bag. "Would you care if I slept out too?" Tony asked.

"Why would I care?" Pete asked. "The outdoors is yours too and big enough for both of us."

They helped Mr. Savala up the steps and took one of the new chairs into the wagon. "You can sit in it while you read the letters," Tony said.

After they'd settled themselves for the night Tony thought of a question which had come into his mind a few minutes before.

"Pete, why did Grandfather tell you about the house on the ranch? Have you thought about renting it? Getting married or something?"

"Not getting married," Pete said. "But maybe something. It's Ascona's business so he should tell. But don't worry. It's a thing he should do — or that's the way I see it. The renter moving out may be a step in the right direction."

Tony had a lot of questions in his mind. They were running around hunting answers. Tony raised up a little and looked across at Pete. *He's asleep already.*

Junie came up to Tony's side, sniffing and wagging his bushy tail. Tony reached out and put his arm around the dog's neck. "Lie down," he whispered. "I've got to get to sleep. We've got us a bunch of work to do tomorrow."

But thoughts kept popping up in Tony's mind. It was as if he had something to figure out before he could sleep.

The soft night wind shook the door of the camp wagon. It made a clapping sound as it hit the wood framework.

Tony turned over and looked toward the sheep pens. As usual, a few lambs were bleating and now and then a mother answered.

"That's what's different," he thought. "The bleating of the sheep doesn't sound bad tonight, not scared, or sad, or noisy. They're safe sounding. Maybe because they know they have a shepherd."

14

The pace of the next three days was faster. Herding sheep with Pete Ariat seemed a lot different to Tony from tending the flock with his grandfather. It wasn't so lonely, and the hours didn't seem ninety minutes long.

Pete didn't stay on one side of the grazing land a half day at a time. He was in the saddle most of the day. He'd patrol the borders of the range and nudge strays into line. Then he'd *churrup* to his horse and ride around to see Tony.

Sometimes Pete came to talk about such things as the Basque Festival. Other times he asked questions about Indianapolis, wanting to know about the speedway and Joe Savala's job.

"I could have gone to college when Joe did," Pete said. "I just didn't want to study that hard."

"Are you sorry now — that you didn't, I mean?" Tony asked.

"Now and then, yes," Pete said. "This business of working for a big outfit's not likely to get me any place. But there's this other thing in my mind, owning a flock of my own like your granddad. Even that has its drawbacks. This is a cold and lonesome place in the winter, especially for one man by himself."

Pete was always on the lookout for rocks and whenever he found one that looked good to him he rode around to show Tony. "I still can't figure out how that thunder egg you found got here. I thought they were found mainly in Idaho."

"Well, you said mainly. That doesn't mean they are all there," Tony said.

"I guess you're right," Pete answered. "You're a bright kid."

Tony began to ride Poco more often. He'd been thinking about trying to saddle Trotter or Poco while Pete was at the camp to show him how. Pete didn't make a guy feel dumb for not knowing things.

The noon meals weren't as good as when Ascona Savala did the cooking, but Tony didn't go hungry. One day they ate canned sausages, potatoes baked in ashes, and leftover chocolate cake.

Tony sat cross-legged with the tin plate between his knees.

"Time sure goes a lot faster with you here, Pete," he said.

"It could be that you're getting used to this country," Pete said. "Did you ever think of that?"

"Well, maybe I am. But it's something else. Granddad doesn't talk — not much anyway."

"It's habit, boy," Pete said. "A man's out here on the range for months on end. He gets out of the practice of talking. Take Ascona. If I know him, and I think I do, he's probably turned things over and over in his mind wondering if you'd be interested in hearing what's on the tip of his tongue."

"But he could talk about Dad. Ask questions or tell me stories about when he was a boy. I'd like to hear things like that," Tony said.

Pete set his hat down lower on his forehead to keep the sun from shining in his eyes. "I can tell you something about why Ascona doesn't talk about Joe."

"Why?" Tony asked. "Is he mad at Dad?"

Pete shook his head. "Just the opposite. He's as proud as any father could be. And if you knew this old sheepherder like I do you'd see the love he has for his son whenever Joe's name is mentioned."

"Then why — "

"It's a hurt. A deep down pain," Pete said.

"Because Dad left Nevada?" Tony asked.

"Not so much because, as *when* he left. I think Ascona *expected* Joe to leave this part of the country and maybe even the state. But within four months after Joe pulled out Ascona's wife died. He couldn't stand the house, the empty rooms. That's when he rented his ranch, bought the used wagon, and added to his flock."

"Do you think he'll ever get over this hurt?" Tony asked.

"Not until he goes back to the place where he started running," Pete said.

"You mean the ranch, back to Winnemucca," Tony said.

"I do," Pete said. "It's too lonely out here. And winters are worse."

"I guess I didn't understand," Tony said.

"Well, it's not easy to see why the other guy limps until you try on his shoe and feel the same pinch."

They went back to patrolling along the edges of the flock. Tony had his grandfather on his mind most of the afternoon. He wished someone would talk him into living at the edge of town. *I wonder if Dad worries about him every winter, like Pete does. Or has Dad sort of forgotten how it is out here?"*

Ascona Savala was taking a loaf of Herders' bread out of the pan when they got back to camp. Tony smelled the freshness before he saw the crusty cross.

Pete scolded Mr. Savala. "You been on that foot too much!"

"No, no," Ascona said. "I kept the knee on a chair."

"I'm not so sure about that," Pete said.

"I can herd now. You can go back to your job."

"Trying to get rid of me, huh. Don't like my work! How about that, Tony!"

Tony dreaded the thought of the time when Pete left, and he didn't think his grandfather was ready to be out on the range all day.

Pete sat down at the table. "Let me tell you something. I'm not leaving until the doctor says you can walk on that foot."

"When will I see a doctor?" Mr. Savala asked. "The trip for supplies will not be made for four more days."

Pete looked out the door. "We still have some daylight left. How about Tony and me riding back to the big camp. I'll borrow a truck or Jeep and take you into Winnemucca in the morning."

"Waiting for tomorrow is better than four more days in a chair," Ascona said.

"Then grab a bite and let's go, boy," Pete said.

"Where will I ride?" Tony asked.

"Behind me," Pete said, "and hold on tight."

Tony was only a little scared. Somehow being with Pete erased fear. And he'd been wanting to see the big camp.

Tony wore his quilted jacket and was glad he did. Pete's horse moved like an easy wind once they were up on the road. The air was like a rushing cool stream. Tony ducked his head behind Pete's wide shoulders and held on tightly to his waist.

The pace slowed down after they'd ridden several miles. The horse picked his way through narrow ravines then along a high bluff of rimrock. He turned into a wider canyon and Tony saw the big camp.

Purple shadows lay over the corrals and the sheds. Instead of one camp wagon there were at least fifteen, which formed a semicircle around a pool where spring water bubbled and gurgled. Dusty trucks and two dirt brown Jeeps were parked by the big sheds.

Tony heard the same sounds as he'd been hearing for days. Now there were several dogs barking and it sounded like a hundred times more sheep bleating. *I wouldn't like that.*

Several men were sitting on the steps of wagons. Someone was singing in Basque.

Pete rode up to speak to a man who had silver white hair. "Will you lend me your Jeep, Garat? To take Ascona to the doctor tomorrow."

Tony knew the man must have said yes or something like that. Pete said, "Thanks, I'd rather ask you than the foreman. This is Joe Savala's boy, Tony. He's getting to be a pretty fair sheepherder."

"Why not?" Mr. Garat said. "It's in the blood."

"We'd better go, after I put my horse in the corral. Say, is my brother in off the range?"

"No," Mr. Garat said. "He was on the north rim. They moved their wagon up there. They'll be in tomorrow sometime."

"Well, if he gets back before I do tell him why my horse is here. I'll bring your Jeep back tomorrow night for sure."

"Don't worry about that," Mr. Garat said. "I'll not have time off for ten days."

As they headed back toward the road Tony asked, "Don't you ever wish you had your own car, Pete?"

"I have one. An old sedan. 1935 model. I keep it in Ascona's shed at the ranch. I work on it a lot. That struggle buggy really shines. I wouldn't drive it in this rough country."

"I'd like to see that ranch before I go back home," Tony said.

"You will, boy," Pete said. "I'll see to that personally."

15

Tony crawled out of his sleeping bag the next morning as soon as he was wide enough awake to smell the coffee. As he walked through the door his grandfather was asking, "What time do you think the doc will be around his office?"

"We'd better be in there before nine," Pete said. "He leaves then to go to houses, I know. I took Julio in when he was cut by the shears. We had to wait three hours."

Tony listened as he ate. "They *have* to say something about the sheep. They surely won't just ride off and leave me. Will they ask me if I want to stay or tell me I have to?"

Pete pushed back his chair and looked at Mr. Savala.

"Do you have questions you wish to ask, Anthony, before we go?" Mr. Savala said.

"You mean about the sheep? You're trusting me to watch them?"

"I don't see why not, or who else," Pete said. "We'll take them to the low sides of the canyon."

"As far away from the coyotes and mountain lions as we can get," Tony thought. "That's what he means."

"We will not be gone more than two hours," Mr. Savala said. "Do as you've done, as you think Pete or I would do."

Pete rode all the way out to the range while Mr.

Savala shaved and dressed.

"We'll go ahead to the tallest grass," Pete said. "That way the sheep will not stray so often."

Tony rode Poco, but he began to wish he'd conquered his fear of the bigger faster horses. The pony might not move swiftly enough to get him to a trouble spot.

Pete dropped the water jug and started to ride off. Then he turned in the saddle and said, "Don't worry about the head of the flock. The lead sheep will manage that end. Listen for that bell and watch the sides."

Pete touched his hand to the brim of his hat and rode off. Tony watched him go. Then he took a long breath and began circling the flock.

He stopped the pony on a slope from which he could see the slowly moving sheep. He slid to the ground and sat with his back to a manzanita bush. He looked up at the ragged peaks that cut into the skyline. Snow powdered the highest places. Clumps of sagebrush were like prickly pillows on the rocky land.

Then he looked to the left. A flash of yellow had caught his eye. Wild canaries were darting in and out of the trembling leaves of an aspen tree.

"I'll never forget this place, how it looks now. But how is it here in winter? Do the birds stay and does the grass stay green? If not, what do the sheep eat?" Tony said to himself.

Tony was deep in thought, trying to picture his grandfather alone in the cold winter months. Then he became aware of a faint bleating. "That's a lamb." He could tell the difference now between the old

"We'll go ahead to the tallest grass," Pete said.

sheep and the young.

He jumped to his feet then listened. The crying sound came from the side closest to the upper levels of the foothills. A lamb had strayed.

Tony climbed on Poco and dug his heels into her fat sides. The pony actually trotted for several yards. Then as they climbed higher she slowed to a fast walk. By then Tony could hear the lamb above the clopping of Poco's hooves, and their scraping on the rocks.

"How'd it get this far so quickly and without me seeing it?" Tony looked back and realized that it was easy for a lamb's movements to be hidden in some places. The tall wavy grass ran up to the edge of a thick row of sagebrush. No one could see the woolly little animal move under the green covering.

Tony saw the lamb ahead. It had run up against a jutting shelf of rock and could go no farther. He slid off Poco's back and picked up the trembling stray.

"How'm I going to get you back to your mother?" Tony said scratching the pointed little face. "I don't have a gunny sack on a saddle like Pete and Grandfather. I don't even have a saddle."

As he turned to walk back to the flock he saw a moving blur of brown on a crag high up in the rimrock wall. He shaded his eyes and saw the mountain lion. It was perched on the peak looking down.

Tony's heart thumped. It beat nearly as fast as that of the lamb which he cradled in his arms. He wasn't afraid for himself. He knew now that the big cats wouldn't come down this far when people were near, at least not in bright sunlight.

But the lamb could have gone farther. "And that's why the coyotes and the mountain lions wait around up there," Tony thought.

He kept a closer watch on the flock after the lamb trotted back to the other sheep. "There's a lot more to this sheepherding business than I thought. You have to know a lot and be on the watch all the time. And a sheepherder doesn't just lock the door and go on vacation like an accountant or engineer. He's got an all the time responsibility hanging around his neck," Tony thought.

The sun was climbing to the top of the sky when Pete rode up to the range.

"Well, we're back," he said.

"What'd the doctor say?" Tony asked. "Can Grandfather throw away his crutch?"

"I'll tell you while we ride back to camp," Pete said. "Let's turn the sheep."

"Turn them? It's only noon. What's — " Tony said.

"I'll tell you that on the way too. Ascona bought some ice cream in town and had it packed in ice. But it won't keep so long. So! We're eating in camp while we make plans."

"Make plans?"

Pete grinned and said, "You're about to explode with curiosity. Your words come out like grains of popcorn in a hot skillet."

The sheep seemed to know it wasn't time to go back to camp. Pete had to whistle often and circle the flock several times to turn them. Junie barked and darted at the flanks of the moving animals to keep them from stopping to eat.

There wasn't a chance for Pete to explain what

was going on until the gate on the pen was fastened.

"What're they going to eat?" Tony asked.

"I'll break open a few bales of hay later," Pete said.

"Then you're staying?"

"In a way. Come on, you'll find out. Your questions will keep. Strawberry ice cream won't."

As they rounded the end of the camp wagon Tony had the answer to one of his questions. He saw his grandfather walking down the steps. He limped a little but the crutch was gone.

As Ascona dipped scoops of ice cream on the tin plates he and Pete told Tony what was happening. Sometimes one didn't wait for the other. Their telling overlapped.

Mr. Savala started the story. "My days on the range are about over, Anthony. There's to be a change while you are here."

"Yep," Pete said. "It's finally soaked through your grandfather's head that there's a better life for him back on the ranch."

"You mean you're moving in?" Tony said.

"Not me. Us," Mr. Savala said.

"That includes me and my brother Paul," Pete added. "We've been trying to buy the land behind Ascona's ranch for a year or more. I closed the deal while the Doc gave your granddad the once over."

"And we're going to live in my house till Pete and Paul build one or either gets married."

"But what about the sheep?" Tony said.

"I'll keep mine. Pete will buy into the flock and add to it."

"And I'll be the herder but not in the old way.

Times change. My brother Paul and I will switch shifts. We're going to try to get a good stand of grass on our land and maybe a part-time job. Then we can move back to one place and quit all this shifting around."

"When are you going to do all this?" Tony asked.

"Before the day is over," Mr. Savala said. Then he reached in the pocket of his gray shirt and pulled out a letter. Tony saw the blue and red border of an airmail envelope.

"From home," he said as he tore open the flap. "Dad wrote this one." He read a few lines then he said, "Oh, man. This is the greatest!"

16

Tony read the message aloud. "Dear Tony and Father: Would you like to have two more summer shepherds for a couple of weeks? We've rented a trailer for a month and should get to Winnemucca a week from Saturday. We leave next Sunday. Jane says for you to put away all your cooking utensils except the Dutch oven. She wants to taste some Herders' bread. We'll be glad to see both of you."

Tony looked at Pete and then at his grandfather. "They think they're surprising *you*. Wait until they hear about the moving," Pete said.

"This is good," Ascona Savala said. "My Joseph will be here to see us in the old home."

"Shouldn't we send word?" Pete said. "If I know Joe he'd drive right through town. He'd be in a rush to get here."

"This is true," Ascona Savala said. "So! We will write. Tony, you say we will meet them at the Basque Hotel. Then we can save the surprise."

"But will they get it?" Tony asked.

"They might not," Pete said. "I tell you! We can send a telegram by the telephone operator when we go into town this afternoon."

"Are we going into town?" Tony asked. "Who's — "

"Who's going to look after the sheep?" Pete said. "My brother. We saw Julio in town. He's taking Paul the word that we're now in business for ourselves."

"Will he come so soon?" Tony asked.

"He'll come. He's been pawing the ground to get off the range part time."

Tony shook his head. "And I thought things never happened out here. It seemed like one day was the same as another."

"A lot of them are," Pete said. "But changes don't exactly come by themselves. People have to make up their minds to act. Right, Ascona?"

Mr. Savala smiled. Then he said, "It is time for more action. We must leave the wagon neat for Paul Ariat."

"You mean we're going to stay at the ranch tonight?" Tony asked.

"We are," Mr. Savala said. "We will need to clean the place. We have fences to mend on my land and his."

"Then I'll take a week of herding and let Paul work and look around for a part-time job."

"Should I pack my things?" Tony asked.

"You should. And I will take what we have room to haul," Mr. Savala said.

By the time Paul Ariat rode up on his horse, leading Pete's, the back of the Jeep was loaded with bags and boxes.

Pete showed Paul where things were kept in the wagon. Mr. Savala drew an outline of the ranges on the ground with a stick. "There is one bad thing," Mr. Savala said. "I cannot make Junie stay. He'd miss me."

"And you'd miss him," Pete said. "Own up."

"Yes, I would. We've been together a long time," Mr. Savala said.

"Don't worry," Paul said. "I can get along. Julio's training a young dog for us."

"I'll leave you my radio," Tony said. "You keep it until I leave Nevada anyway."

As the Jeep climbed up to the road Tony looked back at the canyon. The mountains were still there but they didn't look like a prison wall now. He saw the green of the range, the white caps on the peaks and the sparkle of the sun on the water at the spring.

Tony knew that he'd be back out to the camp. His dad would want to come. *But it won't be the same.*

"You know something," Tony said, "I'm not as glad to leave this place as I thought I'd be. Oh, I still don't hate to go, but it's not been so bad. Not really."

Pete took his hand off the steering wheel and rubbed the top of Tony's head. "If we'd had a few more weeks we'd have made a Basque sheep-herder out of you."

Tony glanced at his grandfather. Was he sad at leaving the range? *He doesn't look sad, sitting there patting Junie and looking straight ahead. I guess Basques are used to leaving places.*

Pete drove straight through town to the ranch.

"There's our stopping place," Ascona Savala said. "See, on the left."

Tony leaned forward and looked. He saw a low house of some kind of gray brick. The roof was red tile and trees shaded a narrow porch which ran across the front.

"Say, that's a neat place," Tony said.

"Neat?" Mr. Savala said. "I see much work to be done."

"Neat is a slang word, Grandfather. It means nice, good, groovy."

Mr. Savala said, "I have enough trouble with the English now. Don't change words on me."

Tony walked through the five rooms. Then he hurried back to the door. "There's furniture!"

"Sure," Pete said. "It's been here all the time."

"I will scrub and you sweep, Tony," Mr. Savala said briskly, "while Pete unloads the Jeep. Your grandmother would weep to see so much dust and spilled food."

Pete grinned. "He's at home," he said to Tony. "I've not heard that tone of voice since he left the ranch. The sad echoes have faded."

Within an hour a fresh clean smell filled the house. As they worked they decided which room would belong to Pete and Paul. Mr. Savala had his own place.

"And Tony can sleep on the daybed in the dining room. It was new when I left here. We will take the blankets out of the locked closet where I stored them. They should be washed. And we need food."

"I know what's itching you," Pete said. "You can't wait to get up town and let your friends know you're back."

Mr. Savala looked at Pete and nodded. "This is true. But there are not as many friends as there were."

"But there are enough for you to swap yarns with and join in Basque songs," Pete said.

"We will eat at the hotel," Mr. Savala said. "Can

we find clean clothes in a hurry? I'll treat you young men."

"We can," Pete said. "Hurry, Tony, before he changes his mind."

As they left the house they saw that sunlight was fading.

"Do you know what we forgot?" Pete said. "We didn't send a telegram."

Suddenly Tony had an idea which came bursting out in words. "Let's call my folks. I'll pay for it."

"Telephone all the way to Indianapolis?" Mr. Savala said. "Wouldn't that cost a lot of money?"

"Not so much," Tony said. "If we wait until after eight, after we eat, night rates are on. It'll be a lot cheaper then."

"I guess it will be all right," Mr. Savala said. "Joseph should be told to stop here. But no more than that. Remember!"

It was nearly eight o'clock and Pete and Tony had not managed to get Mr. Savala out of the hotel dining room. His face was shining as Tony hadn't seen it. His eyes sparkled as he talked with old friends.

Finally Pete said, "Let's find a telephone and leave him here."

As they walked to the lobby Tony said, "I think you were right, Pete."

"About what?"

"About Grandfather's hurt not being healed until he came back to the place where he was when he started running away from things."

"Well, he's back," Pete said. "And here's the pay phone. Do you have change?"

"I think so," Tony said. "I haven't spent a dime since I left this hotel over two weeks ago."

Tony asked Pete to stay near as he placed the call. "I think Dad would like to speak to you."

Tony felt excited as the operator took the number. He didn't hear the click of a lifted receiver until three rings were completed. He'd begun to think no one was at home.

Then he heard his mother's voice say, "Hello."

"Mom. It's me, Tony."

"It *is* — Joe, it's Tony. Oh, it's good to hear your voice. Is something wrong?" Jane Savala asked.

"No. I knew you'd think that!" Tony said. "But we're fine."

"Where are you?"

"We're in Winnemucca. Grandfather wants me to give Dad a message."

"Here he is," Jane said.

"Hi there, Son," Joe Savala said. "Did you get our airmail letter?"

"We sure did," Tony said. "The news is great. That's why I'm calling. You're supposed to stop at the hotel before you go out to the canyon."

"Why?" Joe asked.

"I can't tell you why. But you'll be glad."

"You sound mysterious, Tony. Is there a surprise in the air?" Joe asked.

"There is, and I'm not going to say any more. I'll give it away. Here's someone you haven't heard for a long time. Tell Mom good night."

After Pete talked to his old friend, he and Tony walked outside. The stars were pinpoints of gold in a dark blue sky. The air was still and the town was quiet. No sheep were bleating and no bells tinkled. The sharp yapping of the coyotes was too far away to be heard.

Pete drew a long breath. "It's been a big day. We'd better drag Ascona home. It's time for us sheepherders to go back to the fold."

17

The next week was a time of looking forward. Tony's grandfather kept everyone busy getting ready for the arrival of his son and his wife. He seemed to want the preparations to go on and on. It was as if he was on a path leading to the great day and didn't want to stop for a minute, for fear he might delay the coming.

As soon as one clean-up job was finished he thought of another. Paint brushes slapped against the plaster walls of every room in the house. Rolls of new linoleum were laid in the kitchen and what Ascona called the parlor. The other floors were painted a shade which Pete called pale, wet mud. Ascona said it wouldn't show tracks.

Tony and Pete teased Mr. Savala about being a bossy housekeeper. "He keeps us painting things 'til I'm scared to walk or sit down; afraid I'll stick to something," Pete said two days before the visitors from Indiana were to arrive.

"And besides that," Tony said, "we've walked a hundred extra miles going around the house to other doors so we won't track up stuff."

The three of them were sitting on the narrow porch at sundown. Ascona listened with a half smile on his face. "Sounds like you two are having much trouble. Like maybe you'd rather be on the range."

"Oh, no," Pete said. "No, sir! I take it all back."

Mr. Savala looked up at the sloping roof. "That corner post is falling to pieces. Maybe we can whittle out a new one tomorrow."

"You mean we're not going to paint?" Tony asked.

He was teasing and somehow he felt his grandfather knew it. The two men went on talking and Tony listened for a while. Then he thought about what he'd heard. His grandfather was really great. Here he was, in a way, starting all over again. What was behind was gone, at least for most of the time.

"He's made less fuss about leaving the range than I did over coming here for a month," Tony thought. "He sure has learned to take things as they come."

Tony watched Mr. Savala as he lit his pipe, curling browned fingers around the curved stem. *There's sure a lot for me to learn. Will I ever be like Granddad? Is there enough Basque in me, or enough Savala?*

The house was in order by noon the next day. Every window and door was open to clear the air of the smell of paint. It was impossible to tell what time Tony's parents would pull into town. So the three who were eager to welcome them, dressed in clean clothes, ate dinner at the hotel at noon and waited in the shade of the aspen trees at the east side.

Three retired sheepherders joined them. After a while Tony became restless and he walked up and down looking first one way then the other. He saw license plates from eleven states in the half hour he paced the sidewalk. One was from Indiana.

Suddenly he caught a glimpse of a maroon sedan.

He stopped until he was sure it was his family's car. Then he dashed back to the hotel yelling, "Grandfather! Pete! They're here!"

The next few minutes were filled with greetings and questions and answers. It was a wonder anyone knew who was replying to whose question.

Finally Joe Savala silenced them all by saying, "What's the big mystery! Why were you so set on us meeting you here?"

Tony and Pete smiled at each other then looked at Ascona Savala. He should be the one to answer. They hadn't discussed this matter. They just knew how the other felt.

Mr. Savala squared his shoulders and set his best felt hat back on his head. "We met you here because this is the stopping place. Come on, my son. We are going home."

Joseph Savala looked at his father with a question in his eyes. He read the answer in a motion Ascona made. He pointed back up the street.

"You really mean *home*, don't you!" he said.

"It is time," his father said.

Tony glanced at his mother. Tears filled her eyes. He tried to blink his away.

"You are right," Joe said. "It *is* time and past. Come on, everybody, climb in."

"I'll walk with Father Savala," Jane said. "My legs need limbering."

Pete and Tony rode the three blocks and tried to pour the happenings of the week into a few minutes.

"What I don't see," Joe said, "is what made him decide to do it. I thought he never would."

"It took time," Pete said. "And months and years of loneliness."

"You're leaving out something, Pete," Tony said. "I don't think Granddad would have made the change if you and Paul weren't going in with him."

The next two weeks were like a long family reunion. Pete took his turn on the range and it was Paul who mended fences and built winter shelters for sheep that week.

Jane Savala did all the cooking and had plenty of time to hang curtains at the recessed windows. Tony and his father and grandfather made several trips to the range. One day they drove on to the big camp to see old friends.

As the time of leaving drew near a strange feeling came over Tony. He tried to picture how this place would be with him away. This made him a little sad. It was the same as he'd felt before he left Indianapolis. Was this always the way when you left people you knew and cared about? Did you always want some part of you to stay with them? Or did it?

Three days before the time to go home Joe Savala surprised everyone, even Jane. He came home from a walk over town and said, "Well! It's all settled. I made a call to Indiana. We're going to the Basque Festival. So be prepared. We leave for Elko two days after tomorrow."

"You mean you have an extension on your vacation?" Jane said.

"Two days," Joe answered, "We'll pull the camper and bunk in it. You too, Pete."

"Well, I don't know about that," Pete said. "It'll

101

be my turn to tend sheep."

"Why don't we go out and see Paul. Maybe he'll let you and Tony and me take over two days. Make a trade. Or would you rather stay here, Son?"

Tony looked at his grandfather. It'd be OK to live in the camp wagon with Pete and his dad. And he wished he could find another thunder egg. But he'd soon be gone.

"I think I'll stay," he said. "Grandfather promised to take me out to the old rustler's hideout, and out around Independence Valley." Tony had heard, in the talk around the campfire, that the first Basque to come to Nevada had settled in this valley.

Mr. Savala nodded. "That is true. I made the promise. Tony should see that place." He was pleased. Tony could tell.

The trip to Elko was a gay holiday. Sections of the streets were filled with dancers in gay costumes of red and green and white. Visitors sat on long benches and joined in singing and hand clapping. Many boots stomped to the rhythm of the music.

Weight-lifting and wood-chopping contests were held at one end of the town. Tony asked Pete why he didn't enter the competition. "Not me," Pete said. "As a kid I was sure I'd be an ax-wielding champion. But now I'm a part of the changing west. If I had to cut much wood I'd get me a chain saw."

Basque came from every state in the far West and townspeople and tourists added to the crowd. Pete told Tony, "This is the one time in the year when some of these people get to town."

"People like Paul, you mean?" Tony asked.

"Don't worry about Paul. I'm scooting back tonight. He'll get here for the wind-up."

There was very little conversation on the way back to Winnemucca. They were all tired and they knew the time for parting was near. There was an unspoken feeling that they were easing into separation. The Joe Savalas would be heading northeast early the next morning, leaving the rimrock of the Sierra Nevadas and going toward the flatlands of central Indiana.

Pete said good-bye as soon as they pulled up in front of the house. He shook hands with Jane and slapped Joe's shoulder. Then he turned to Tony. Even in the moonlight Tony could see Pete's wide grin. "Well, young friend! Our paths part for now. But who knows? I may try to find Indiana one of these years."

"I hope you do, Pete," Tony said. "Try hard."

"And I'll keep my eye out for another thunder egg," Pete said. He tipped his rolled rim hat and strode toward the Jeep he'd bought the week before.

Tony took a deep breath. He couldn't forget Pete. Even if he never saw him again. The tall lean sheepherder was a part of his life, like the foothills, the wild canaries, the tall pines, and the tinkling bell on the lead sheep.

The Savalas sat on the porch until the cooling air drove them inside. Jane tried again to coax Ascona to go back with them.

"Not now," the sturdy man said. "It is good to be with family. And it *is* fine to know my grandson. A pretty good shepherd, this Tony! But visits are better if there are spaces between. I have decided.

He couldn't forget Pete.

I'll be in your place at Christmas."

Tony felt good and sad at the same time. He had this feeling a lot during these four weeks. Good feelings had gradually crept in to take the place of loneliness and homesickness and anger.

He looked out and up at the rim of mountains against the sky. Junie whimpered in his sleep. Did he miss the sounds of the sheep?

"Maybe I wouldn't feel sad about leaving if I still hated this place," Tony thought. "But I'm glad I don't."

The Author

Dorothy Hamilton was born and lives in Delaware County, Indiana. She received her elementary and secondary education in the schools of Cowan and Muncie, Indiana. She also attended Ball State University, Muncie, and has taken work by correspondence from Indiana University, Bloomington, Indiana. She also has attended professional writing courses at various times.

Mrs. Hamilton grew up in the Methodist Church and participated in numerous school, community, and church activities until the youngest of her seven children was married.

Then she was led by prayer-induced direction into service as a private tutor. In a real sense this service was a mission of love. More than 190 girls and boys have come to Mrs. Hamilton for gentle encouragement, for renewal of self-esteem, and to learn to work.

The experience of being a mother and a tutor inspired Mrs. Hamilton in much of her writing. She worked in a ten-day preschool session for children of migrant workers at Mt. Summit, Indiana. She is deeply empathetic toward children whose homes are widely scattered.

Seven of her stories have been published by quarterlies, including the Ball State University *Forum*. One story, "The Runaway," was nominated for the American Literary Anthology. She has had published thirty-four serials, fifty-five short stories, and several articles in religious publications since February 1967. She has written for radio and newspapers. She is author of *Anita's Choice* (1971), *Christmas for Holly* (1971) and *Charco* (1971).